Two Apart

Angela - the bride

enjoy - where ever you are

love ya :-)

D G Hunter

ISBN: 1500166707
ISBN 13: 9781500166700

Celebrating the cowboy in all of us
and
the companionship of horses.

Preface

The imagination is a wonderful gift from God. Look around and see creative genius at work on an incomprehensibly grand scale.

This fictional piece is forged from the desire to express vividly in words what is visible. Particular scenes were manifested in the mind's eye as mirror-images of what has been witnessed or experienced. Each character possesses a certain personality and is given a history to define his or her behavior.

The reader is encouraged to research the historical events that serve as a background for each character's origin. The exploration of the Revolutionary War, the Civil War, the impact on progress brought about with the expansion of the railroad, and even the Haitian Revolution that began in 1791 sets the scene for the landscape as well as the manners displayed by each character. These significant chapters in history as well as immigration had direct influence in orchestrating the independence, and the ultimate nationalization of the United States between the Atlantic and the Pacific oceans.

Insight into the lives of immigrants allows a better understanding of the diversity of the individuals who are collectively Americans. It is important to appreciate the fact that our heritage and ancestry lie outside the borders of our country, but we are not bound to philosophies, doctrines, or ideologies practiced in any other country nor adverse regulations imposed by foreign governments. We are Americans first and foremost, a democracy sharing in a wealth of liberties, governed with the Constitution that protects our nation's citizens from tyrants and kings.

Religious freedom was the basis upon which the New World was colonized. It was an important foundation for the lives of the common populace but was soon exploited by those who desired to rob vulnerable people of their possessions as well as their souls.

Selfish ambition was the driving force behind the greedy self-proclaimed entrepreneurs toting bags made from carpet remnants. They looted the property of war-weary and destitute families left to ruin in the wake of oppression.

The heart of a nation is resilient and presses ever forward to a better future, overcoming the obstacles set before it. The adventurous spirit dares to step out the door and seeks to discover what is possible beyond the boundaries laid neatly at the edge of the frontier.

Friendship and camaraderie are not defined by color nor status, but by a desire to be part of relationships based on honesty and genuine trust, that sometimes requires faith when it doesn't make sense.

I

The flicker of the small fire danced in shadows on the wall of sandstone that towered above it. Clouds shrouded the night sky. The moon would be full but had not yet risen to illuminate the land. The stand of trees offered cover to any who would otherwise be discovered in the vast plain. James had felt an ill-boding presence on the ride out of the small town many miles back this morning, a feeling that he couldn't shake. He crouched in the deep shadow of the underbrush and mahogany trees, searching his memory for some reason to explain this uneasiness that rose inside of him. He had few friends and depended on no one, but had no enemies who came to mind. His horse stood quiet and still but alert to any movement. He had known this horse from foaling, and many times such as this, he had relied on his companion to speak a silent warning of peril. Even now, making no sound, the stud pricked his ears at something moving toward the camp.

Forgetting the past for now, James focused on what was beginning to unfold before him. He had carefully laid his bedroll by the fire and prepared for whatever was to come. The flames continued their dance, embers popping into the air and flittering on the breeze only to extinguish and drift away. It was then that a man slunk from the shadows and stepped into the firelight. With quiet stealth, the stocky figure crept toward the bedroll. He raised a thick, heavy blade from its sheath and, with one swift lunge, buried it deep into what appeared to be a man lying asleep. Realizing his blunder, looking this way and that, the assassin backed silently but quickly away from the camp, disappearing into the darkness.

The only sound left was the whisper of fluttering, dry autumn leaves and the fire crackling gaily, dancing with the breeze. Again, James tried to recall anyone he had perhaps offended. No one came to mind. In the town last night, he had stopped at the saloon for a quick drink and then gone to the livery to sleep. He preferred those accommodations to any hotel.

The barroom had been filled with heavy smoke and the stench of stale beer and liquor. Spittoons, reeking of rotten tobacco and spit, lined the floor of the bar. James had surveyed the room before entering to acquaint himself with the lay of it and the position of each fellow. At a glance he knew how many tables there were, where the back door was, and even where the barkeep might stash the shotgun for easy reach. Most of the men were cowhands, he supposed. He didn't know what day it was, but he thought it must have been just after payday: most of the men were of the jovial sort—except, he remembered, the three men at the table closest to the door with "PRIVATE" etched in the wood. He remembered them only because they had begun to fidget when he stepped through the swinging doors. One of them had tipped his hat as if to acknowledge an acquaintance. James hadn't responded but went to the bar as if he didn't notice it. They weren't familiar to him. Their unkempt appearance and sunburned faces spoke of long days in the saddle followed by short nights of rest. Thurman, who had gestured to James, squinted as he took a long drag from his crudely rolled cigarette, blowing the smoke into the air from the corner of his mouth. James had positioned himself at the bar so the reflection in the soot-stained mirror would warn him of their intentions. He took note that they returned to their card game but seemed to focus their attention on him. With a quick swig of whiskey, he had taken up his rifle and turned toward the door. He'd paused, and a hush filled the room as he looked again at the men and backed out of the saloon into the street. He heard a chair scratch the wood floor, and at once, the shrill plinks of the piano could be heard resounding over the lively debates and senseless chatter. He had moved quickly to the darkened alley and made his way to the livery.

He came west after the war seeking a simple life, as others before him. His folks had passed on and left him alone. The hills of the frontier had become perilous since he'd lost his family's farm. Everything was gone—all his possessions except his horse, his weapons, and whatever he carried with him in saddlebags.

Though James never served on either side of the conflict, he'd had the important task of crafting the firearms used by the military. Through experience, he was a smith, master of the trade. He knew weapons better than most, even though he was twenty-five (considered young by some accounts). When he had been a boy, his father taught him about the tools that were imperative to everyday life, including a good rifle. He had learned that the slightest detail in any situation was relevant. He now noted the most trivial things that would go unnoticed by others.

As an apprentice, he had excelled in weaponry, becoming a meticulous craftsman. He was handy with a rifle as well as a revolver. He kept both close at hand. A sharp-edged blade was sheathed at his side for quick, easy reach. He had perfected the art of reloading, testing each cartridge for quality and precision. The reproducible capability of the subsequent loads was verified and logged. He didn't claim to be a fast draw. James was, however, deadly accurate.

His father had had several heavy-boned thoroughbred mares that were bred to his uncle's stud. They were intelligent and kind in heart, swift but durable. The colts had been sold to the army to help keep the farm. As far back as he could remember, James had helped his mother care for the foals and had begun their training at an early age. He was proud of his folks and had grieved inconsolably at their passing. He had been given the horse that stood beside him as a gift. That was six years ago—or had it been so long?

He often thought of the past in times of need, for the lessons learned proved invaluable for his survival. Besides, most of his memories were pleasant and worthy of recall. But at this moment, in the dark, beyond the safety of the camp, a twig snapped startling him back to the present. No other sound was heard for the rest of the night. Still he kept vigilant watch. The fire died away with a wisp of smoke rising, dissipating in the crisp fall air. The moon did rise, at last, peeking through the slow-moving fingers of lingering clouds. A stinging, cold breeze whirled around James's face.

The red cliffs and distant horizon began to take shape. At first light, he packed his things, mounted the dark bay stud, and eased along the ledge, keeping a close eye on his trail. They trotted quietly up the draw, being careful to stay below the skyline. There was nothing he could do about the tracks his horse left in the soft, sandy soil, yet he tried to ride where the ground was rockier. He rode till the sun rose overhead, then stopped to rest and graze his horse. He crawled up the knoll and lay flat to survey the land to which he would go.

He cast his gaze upon a panoramic vista of a golden grassland, boundless, spreading in every direction until it faded beyond sight into the distant pale blue sky. The breeze blew the grass tops and rolled across the prairie like waves on the ocean. The stem shafts shimmered and glistened in the noon day sun. The brushing sound changed pitch in the gusting wind. He quickly regained his senses when a hawk shrieked and soared away. He decided that he should turn south and reach the railroad. He felt that foreboding presence again, so he quickened the pace. His horse, seeming to understand the urgency, loped freely.

Nightfall came without incident. This night he kept a cold camp, chewing on the jerked meat he had brought from an outpost across the Great River. His horse munched the grass but stayed close. When he awoke in the morning, the frosty air lay low in the draws and fens. No birds chirped, and the grass lay still, motionless. Yet, the sun rose warm in a clear blue sky. He maintained a southwest course, hoping to reach the railroad before sunset. The land was now flat, with no low-lying washes in which to find cover. It made the uneasy feeling more intense.

He thought about the old man he had found in an alley a while ago. He recalled how haggard and tired he looked. The man was downcast but clear minded. At one time, James thought, this man had been a gentleman or at least shared in the wealth of a noble class. The man showed him a map drawn, he claimed, by some famous explorer whose name he couldn't remember. Why the man offered it to him was a mystery. Pulling it now from his vest pocket, he tried to trace his trail to this point so far. The old man had spent a good deal of time teaching him to read the strange curves and distorted circles that were drawn there. Some of the lines had faded, making the interpretation more questionable. But still, he felt confident in what he saw around him when compared to the map. It was strange, he thought, that he didn't even know the man's name.

The day passed, with clouds beginning to gather in the west. A cold wind gusted and swirled; the grassy plain repeated the melancholy song he had listened to yesterday. There were groves of black walnut trees where he took rest now and then. His shadow lengthened as he rode ever southward. The setting sun trimmed the clouds with pink and orange hues. He decided to ride longer into the darkness and change his direction a little, so as to elude anyone who might be pursuing him.

Nothing broke the silence of the night except the occasional howl of the prairie wolf. There was the distant response of another, then all was silent. At the darkest hour an owl hooted begging for an answer, none came. He wished he'd found the rail line but somehow felt safe where he was, in a deserted place with dark night to cover him. He slept well.

He woke just before the light of the new day. The moon had risen late but still shone bright. Where was his horse? A rush of dread swept through him as he searched for the stud. There had been nothing in the night that had interrupted his slumber. Was he just becoming too complacent? He would remedy that right now. But first, he had to find his horse. Searching the ground for tracks and bent grass, he found himself walking north on an old game trail. This was not what he'd had in mind, but he thought, perhaps the horse was only looking for a watering hole. The fresh hoof prints were easy to follow, and he soon came to a creek that seemed to come up from nowhere. The water was clear and cold. He took a long drink, realizing he hadn't tasted water this good for a long time. He relaxed when the stud quietly nickered to him from a little way up the draw. He scolded the bay. Patting his neck, James tried to suppress the anxiety he felt for his own negligence.

They walked back to camp where he saddled up and continued to ride south. At about midday, there was a wisp of smoke in the distance that seemed to puff along a designated route. It had to be the railroad. Relieved at the sight, he spurred his horse to a lope to the top of the rise.

The tracks stretched across the vast prairie from horizon to horizon. The train he had seen was chugging east. It would do no good to catch that one, he thought. There had to be a town somewhere along the route, so he continued on the westward course, being careful to stay a short distance from the sight of the tracks.

It was nearly three o'clock, as best as he could reckon, when he rode into a settlement beside the rail line. His first stop was the livery, to give his horse a much-needed rest. The stable hand generously offered a large stall wherein the stud could lie down in fresh straw. He offered to check the shoes and was willing to reset them if necessary. The man seemed to recognize a weary traveler, perhaps because he had seen many drifters passing through town. He seemed trustworthy. A price was agreed upon, and included accommodations for both horse and rider. Then James went to the bathhouse to clean up after the long ride.

It had been many days since he had bathed. It felt good. He decided to get a good meal before turning in. At the end of the street was an eating establishment that seemed busy. He went in and ordered a cup of coffee. The menu was simple. It read, "Supper is fried chicken, potatoes, and apple pie for dessert." It sounded good to him, since his last several meals had been jerky and stale cakes. He would stock up on more jerky before pressing on.

Later he passed the only saloon in town. He did, however, look over the swinging doors. The revelers were dancing and singing with a new-fangled player piano. He surmised the room was filled with local patrons. The conversations were robust, with occasional outbursts of laughter. It eased his mind a little, but he avoided the commotion and headed to the livery.

On the third day in this town, he began to feel restless, and the need to move on welled up inside him. He went to the café for one last full meal, determined to leave after dark under the cover of the moonless night. There arose a nervousness inside him that he couldn't shake.

When he returned to the stable, he noticed three more horses standing, weary and soaked with sweat. They were still saddled. These, he thought, had been pressed hard and long. He shook his head as he turned to leave. Then the liveryman shuffled in, grumbling to himself, and unsaddled the first horse. The stable hand, followed close behind and began brushing and cooling it. James asked the old man about the men who owned those horses.

The liveryman said he'd never seen them before, but that they'd been intent on finding out who rode the dark bay stud. They were a reckless bunch, impolite and vulgar. The stableman didn't like them and had given them no information that would give away any identity. With that news, James asked the old man for refuge in a shed just beside the livery. He could still watch the comings and goings about the stable but keep his own position secret.

The next train west was due in a few days. The stableman told him there was a water tank approximately five miles away. The train always stopped there before proceeding westward. James decided he'd board the train there. The stableman made the necessary arrangements. The young stable hand was sent to the mercantile to fill the list of provisions. With that, James said good-bye with gratitude, still bewildered by the three men who pursued him.

He rode out of town under the cover of night and set up camp near the water tank to wait for the train. He had stocked up on coffee, jerked meat, and fresh cakes to last for a week. He would miss this town. Everyone had been friendly and eager to make him feel welcome. Maybe someday he could settle down somewhere like this.

His horse was rested and seemed eager to move on. He settled into an easy gait, tugging at the bit.

II

Winter had been especially harsh. The trees in the orchard had frozen, and even now they stood as lifeless forms with twisted branches. It was a time of change when the young Atwells had packed their belongings on the crude wagon to move to a land of opportunity. They were expecting a child in the fall. It made the journey more arduous. But springtime brought renewed hope, even to the fainthearted, and rich farmland was available to the west.

Two brothers, Norris and Elam Atwell, had set out before the apple trees began to blossom, in search of a better life. What they found was prime land for crops and a brighter future for them all in a remote wilderness. Hard work lay before them, but they were young and able. An older brother, David, had stayed behind, not interested in farming but fascinated by weaponry. Their parents were disappointed in the choices their sons made but wished them well. There was a grand feast the night before they parted with singing at the piano, prayer, and card playing. Farewells were short and without ceremony. The adventurous ones were off before daybreak and the chirping of the birds.

They had planned to buy what land they could and build upon their investment as the years passed. At first it was difficult to make the purchase, because most of the land was given to loyal advocates as payment for service during the Revolution. But with a gift from their father, each man was able to purchase forty acres to begin with. Their tracts were separated by dense woods but were still relatively close together. The only problem they would face was the distance from the nearest township.

It was during the first snowfall of that year that James and Thomas had come into this world of challenge and uncertainty. They were born only moments apart but grew to be opposite in nature, yet, their distinguishing traits complimented one another. Norris and Mary rejoiced, giving no thought to the struggles ahead.

The Atwell farms spread along the edge of the frontier. The children never seemed to notice the hardships the family faced. There were a few skirmishes with ill-mannered misfits, which made everyone more wary of the infrequent traveler. Rumors and disagreeable opinions began to pass through the homesteads. Discontent was looming, and the question of loyalties emerged. Soon the skirmishes worsened, with more insolent men pressing their philosophies upon the quiet settlements of the frontier.

At the age of fifteen, the boys returned to live with their grandparents until the frontier was once again safe. Their grandfather was well known locally as Preacher Eustis. He had built a following by reciting scripture and demanding, with a heavy hand, that the congregation repent of all their faults, whether or not they had any. He was a stern man even at home. The boys were expected to rise early every morning and attend to chores before breakfast. They learned self-discipline and respect for authority, working hard and staying out of trouble for fear of punishment that was carried out in the shed. Grandmother was a kind woman, gentle in spirit. She welcomed the boys with open arms, teaching them their letters, and raising them to respect honesty, truth and the right of fair play. Living by the "Golden Rule" they understood the rewards and consequences of the choices they made. Being very familiar with the Bible they had memorized key verses that seemed to be the continuous theme of all the Preacher's sermons.

They took up an apprenticeship with their uncle David. It was there that they too became obsessed with the power of weaponry. One, however, also found the power of the pulpit and chose to preach fire and brimstone, following in the footsteps of Grandfather.

Discussions of insignificant opinions turned to arguments, and after a time, the two brothers spoke very little, out of respect for their grandmother. She worried over them and seemed more frail as time passed.

The Preacher died suddenly in the pulpit one Sunday morning, clutching his chest and falling lifeless to the floor. In that particular sermon, he had spoken softly and looked often to heaven, speaking of forgiveness and grace. Grandmother's eyes welled with tears as she ran to her husband's side. Her devotion was enduring, even to her death a few short months later. The boys moved into their uncle's home. Preaching remained in the family, however. It seemed as though the Preacher had been reincarnated in a man fifty-three years younger. Thomas had grown in stature and confidence. The small congregation rallied behind him and grew in number, but the opinions of men ultimately divided the house of God. Thomas, who was known as the "Parson," moved on with no words for his brother.

At age eighteen, James, longing for the warmth of home, left his job at the arms company to return to his family's farm. His uncle supplied him with as many provisions as could be stowed in the saddlebags. He would be missed. The boy had a keen sense of precision and was accurate within millimeters. With regret, his uncle bid him farewell, turned, and walked away. The boy spurred his horse down the road, sadly leaving the comfort of his uncle's home.

He was eager, however, to return to the frontier and be with his family again. Yet, all was not as well as he had expected. His mother, weary and worn, was ill and struggled to complete her chores. His father had been wounded when a ruffian attempted to steal a horse. He was unable to overcome the infection. James was glad he had come home.

It was autumn. The mares were with foals. The farm had been neglected, so James set about cleaning the barnyard and putting up the hay for the horses before the winter snowfall. Harnesses needed mending, weeds had to be cleared from the garden, and fences required repair.

That was the year his uncle Elam's stud died suddenly. The army had purchased horses from another farm. The foals in the spring wouldn't bring much. James's father promised him the first stud colt to be born as gratitude for his loyalty and hard work.

His mother died soon after his return, and then, after Norris's leg was amputated, he succumbed to the infection shortly after his wife's death. There alone, James wept in grief he never would experience again.

The winter proved to be long. He had sold a few of the mares and given the rest to his uncle Elam on the other side of the woods. At least the very best of the herd would stay in the family. It was out of one of these mares that he hoped to claim the gift his father had promised.

Word spread quickly about the demise of yet another homestead family. Carpetbaggers from afar came in the spring to lay claim to possessions left behind by the deceased. The rumors of war began to be a cause of great concern. Many of these frontiersmen knew little of the disagreements of the elite groups living in luxury along the coastal regions. But war did indeed reach even their front doors.

After the death of Norris, Elam moved his family farther west, away from the reckless conflict. Some called it cowardly, but he was getting up in years and needed to safeguard a family with sons still too young to understand the complexities of death and destruction without reason. He took the few mares left in the herd to begin anew. The going was slow because of the greater accumulation of household items and some other livestock.

James, nearly twenty and considered a man, returned to his uncle at the firearms company taking the mare and her colt he had claimed for his own. He felt quite certain he would be offered a job during these perilous times. He stayed to the backcountry and rode at night as much as possible to avoid contact with any strangers.

It took him three weeks to reach his uncle. They sat at the table while James spoke of the hardships his family was enduring. His words painted a vivid picture of hope, however dim it seemed in his own mind. He spoke of the heaven-reaching mountains clad in the deep verdant green pines, their scent wafting in the breeze after a misty rain. No words could describe the sound of the wind blowing through the pendulous boughs of the ageless trees. The water of the streams was so clear and cold that the depths of the soul would be cleansed upon drinking of it. Thirst would be quenched, yet the lips would crave all the more the burning of ice-cold water.

His thoughts and concerns turned in yet another direction. He asked his uncle for news of his brother. According to letters and hearsay, he had gone farther south engaging in biblical debates with anyone who would give him audience. There was none better at arguing the validity of both sides of a topic. He was notorious for beginning on one side of the issue only to conclude with the relevance of the opposite side. There were some who thought he would somehow end up in the political arena. He was considered by others to be twisted and lawless for the unreasonable notions that surrounded him. He had been run out of town a time or two by those who tired of pandering words with a would-be preacher toting more than just a Bible; it may have been coincidence, but it also seemed that a horse would be missing after his hasty departures.

Nonetheless, his letters came from various postal stations. The last one had been received two or three months ago. The postmark was from somewhere southwest, near the frontier. It had taken a month to reach the northern region of civilization. As the conflict of opinions escalated, news from southern stations stopped altogether. There were no more letters.

James returned to his job with the gunsmith. He became more dedicated to the building of fine rifles and developing formulas for accurate, consistent ammunition. He would spend long hours testing different powders and weights of lead shot at the shooting range behind the factory. The soldiers who were stationed to protect the factory attested to the quality of the firearms he produced. His name became legendary, with his initials etched in each barrel. His endorsement alone sold many rifles to civilians as well as the military. The work continued for five years. He longed for peaceful freedom and at last, the end of conflict.

A war that divided the young nation ended with surrender and the death of a great leader—some would say. Others were of a mind that it was a bittersweet victory and still felt no lasting satisfaction. There would be animosity for many years to come. Would the deep wounds of the heart ever be healed?

III

The young preacher, known only as Tom Parson—for many did not know his true name—had charisma that could lull even the angels into believing his interpretations of the "Good Book." He had taken his grandfather's place, his heart intent on seeking the justice of absolute truth. He had been determined to save every soul in the small church, as his grandfather had tried to do. After two years, however, he grew all the more impatient with the men of the congregation as the conflicts of the nation grew worse. Opinions among the parishioners began to clash. The very truth was being compromised to keep order. His sermons began to flare with condemnation for those who were considered rebellious. He had been willing to allow everyone into the house of God, while others hadn't been. Dissension grew within the brotherhood, breaking the trust that had so long been present. What would Grandfather have done? In a raging sermon one Sunday morning, the young parson denounced the congregation as heretics. At that, he was forced out of town, dodging the flurry of bullets as fast as his horse could gallop.

Realizing that burning bridges could never again be crossed, he was compelled ever southward. He was a good man at heart, but along with his charm he was very compulsive and quick tempered. He never returned. Alone, he pressed on.

He was not poor and helpless when he left, however. In his shrewdness, he had made off with a fairly large sum of the parish's collections. It was the first time he had stolen anything. A wave of guilt swelled into his conscience, but passed quickly, since he would probably find himself at the end of the hangman's noose if he attempted to return.

At the next settlement, he penned a letter to his uncle, notifying him of his intention to continue south and find a new life in the pulpit. Promising to keep in touch, he rode farther from his roots and deeper into a troubled land. He was not sympathetic to any opinion of persuasive policy. He sought only to help the innocent endure the discord that seemed to grow in strength on both sides. It was as if two dragons aflame, poisoned with greed and seething jealousy, were devouring the very treasure that both equally possessed. What would be left when nothing but evil was poured out on the land? It would become desolate, barren, and void of substance, incinerated into an uninhabitable waste.

He found communities of ordinary people seeking answers to the calamity that had befallen them. Some were still unaware of what was happening and why. He brought them comfort and renewed hope. However, northern armies invaded these settlements, dashing their dreams of peace and safety. The parson led the remnant of his congregation to safe havens, looking back only to see the smoke of destruction left in the wake of savage zealots. Rain began to fall. A chill fell over the small company moving slowly through the dense forest.

These people persevered under the weight of natures wrath. Even in the face of devastation, they found strength to shelter their loved ones from the elements that seemed to curse the whole land. They gathered boughs and twigs to build simple huts under the spreading branches of the great evergreens. The men were skillful hunters and soon returned with venison for all. The future looked grim, but they passed the days going about the business of living. Meetings were held regularly to encourage and strengthen everyone's resolve to survive.

Traveling farther into the southern wilderness, weak and weary, they at last came to an outpost where they were welcomed and tended to. This place had not yet felt the bruises of the conflict. These people were, however, preparing themselves for the inevitable. There had been news from ever deeper in the south that a military of rebellion was pressing all men into service, yet, this small settlement had remained secluded, avoiding the grip of the involuntary enlistment.

The Parson stayed on as a spiritual advisor. His sermons offered words of everlasting salvation without the comfort of physical rewards. The sun rose to begin a bright new day. The air was once again fresh, with misty dew dripping from every blade of grass. The people went about their chores, content for the time being. Still, their hearts were heavy with the fear of impending peril.

After a time, however, another traveling preacher happened into the settlement. He began persuading the people to follow *his* deluded message. The settlement was soon entrenched in arguments about church doctrine as this new biblical ambassador convinced the community to compromise, yet again, on the truth. His interpretations of the written word became gospel, and he forced those who didn't share his viewpoint out of the settlement.

This time, reasoning got Tom Parson nowhere, and before the blaze of guns, he escaped retribution astride a great thoroughbred that was not his own. He had stolen for a second time. Riding long into the night, he bore no remorse this time. He was angry at being bested by someone who knew less than he did. He mused at the cunning that man had possessed. Shaking the dust from his boots, he vowed that it would happen no more.

He remained devoted to the truth, though he took greater care in choosing words to ease the burdens that smother the joy of daily living. His sermons were consistently laced with the assurance that soul saving grace is obtainable, yet he soon learned that vulnerable people would attend meetings to hear words that would make them feel good about themselves and justify their meager existence. He became a traveling Bible thumper, toting two books, one carrying the words of life, the other a .45-caliber revolver. He passed the collection plate halfway through his sermons, since at the end he had to flee from those who disagreed with him.

He too became frustrated with the sweeping conflict that gripped a land once enchanting and beautiful beyond description. Screams of anguish followed distant rumbles of cannon fire, and wails of despair drowned out the jubilant shouts of victory. By stealth, a little bit of faith, and a lot of luck, he made his way back to his home in the northern regions of the frontier. He penned one more note. It simply stated, *"Life in a hopeless land must prevail."*

When at last he came to the homestead he had left at age fifteen, grief consumed him. Gone were the rolling hayfields and the rows of corn he and his brother had played in. The foundation of the house lay tangled in ivy, with splintered and burnt timbers strewn about, as evidence that an explosion had dismantled it. The chimney stood crumbling and black. Love for life left him in despair. In the midst of ashes, he wept bitterly.

In the quiet stillness of the morning he came to his senses, realizing the road he now trod would lead only to his own death and destruction. His heart was filled with remorse at his despicable behavior, as he saw it. He felt unworthy of pardon for his failings that now lay bare. Calling on his faith he was reminded that each day offers the resolve to endure life's challenges and promises of a new beginning. He was determined to explore the chance to right the wrongs he had wrought by his own self-serving choices.

He had to find his uncle Elam. Perhaps in the family he would find strength and healing for his downtrodden spirit. Pulling a flask from his coat he took a long draft to warm his body. His inquiries concerning his uncle's whereabouts led some to suggest that Elam had moved his family farther west. Thomas headed down the road his uncle had taken three years before.

The parson couldn't stay out of debates, biblical or otherwise. The farther west he traveled, the more he encountered people who would not tolerate that sort of conversation. Most of the discussions deteriorated into shouts of opposition, regressing into brawls after shots of whiskey fueled the belligerent opinions all the more. He knew better than to preach to a drunken rabble, but always defended his position, either with words of wisdom or the folly of the .45.

At one particular roadhouse, the logic of wisdom gave way to disastrous folly. It was by coincidence that four brothers had stopped, weary from travel, to ease the soreness of the saddle. Being contemptuous, and seeing the Bible, they began harassing the tall man in the long black coat sitting at the table. He too was weary from travel and intolerant. There was soon a standoff. One of the four was killed. Thomas fled. "I have to find another line of work," he mused.

Near the reaches of the Great River, Thomas found his uncle. The family was a hearty lot. His aunt, a robust woman, was strong in body and conviction. His uncle was heavier than he had remembered. Still, the twinkle in his eye brought back the pleasant memories of yesterday when life was easy to decipher, free of the encumbrance of sorrow, greed, and envy. His cousins were excited to see this man of great stature and favor in their eyes. They listened to his tales of adventure with awe. He had traveled so far, it seemed to them. In this home, he finally found peace. The anger that had been pent up for so long melted away. He began to think clearly about the important matters once again.

He had never taken charity. He rose early each day and tended to chores that would ease the burden of his presence, though his loving aunt never saw him as such. His uncle welcomed the strength of a young man and graciously accepted the relief of another pair of strong hands. The weight of the day rolled from their shoulders, bringing a renewed spirit to the small farm. In the evening, there was now time for scripture reading, gospel music, and laughter in this home as in times past. Even the land seemed to blossom and become more fruitful. Maybe it was just the radiance of the new spring, or perhaps something much deeper. The mares began to foal. With each new birth, the future seemed brighter. These horses were the lifeblood of the family—hope and strength.

That summer, Thomas and his uncle rode together to search for and purchase a stud to replace the great sire that had died a few years before. Both men knew good horseflesh. The knowledge of each complemented that of the other as they looked for strength, athletic ability, stamina, and a gentle spirit—a stallion sound in every element. This horse's offspring were to be companions as well as a means of transportation. Big-boned thoroughbreds were what the

Atwells looked for. The mares they owned were good-natured horses with large round feet and good conformation. The stud was to be strong willed and confident. The name he bore must be regarded with high esteem among the industry of the time.

The colt they chose was lean and had a kind eye. The men knew he would grow into his long legs. He had a heavy hindquarter, long shoulder, straight legs, and round feet like his mother's. They were confident in their selection. With this two year old stallion, they made their way home to the edge of the frontier.

In the beginning the young stud was willful, bred with the stubborn spirit of self-preservation. However, with persistence and patience, Thomas prevailed in subduing the stallion's natural resistance to training, developing a bond of trust. The offspring of such a fine sire were precious indeed.

Buyers soon flocked to the farm to purchase some of the finest horses on the frontier. Horse racing had become a pastime of the elite. Many of the colts went to stables in the east and performed as expected. The stud became known as Against All Odds, since many of his colts outran the competition with better odds at the betting booths.

One day, a man from farther west came to the farm in search of these horses. He chose two fine yearlings and a gray mare to add to his family's herd. His family had stocky horses that ran fast and were agile but lacked the stamina for long distance. The buyer's father wanted to incorporate the endurance of the thoroughbred into the toughness of a short-distance runner. The price and delivery were agreed upon. Thomas was to deliver the horses via railroad in October of that year.

His uncle knew of a man with a map of this new country in a town southwest of the homestead who was confident in his claim of knowing explorers west of the river. Elam sent a message to this man with a description of Thomas, who would come for the map.

The time had come to begin the trip to deliver the horses. With the colts, Thomas set out on a new quest, riding the gray mare to the Great River and the railroad.

He headed to the settlement intent on finding the man with the map and staying out of trouble—an obligation to his aunt. However, he sought out the first saloon that bustled with activity. He inquired of the man his uncle had sent him to find. No one could recall who this fellow was. Thomas continued to ask around concerning this man, since without a map, it would be difficult to find his way. Finally, he asked the local law enforcement for assistance. The deputy directed him to the cemetery. Rumor had it that the man Thomas sought had succumbed to the elements one dark night as he lay in the alley behind the livery. There were no witnesses and no evidence to point to any wrongdoing, so the investigator's report indicated. After all, he had been a dismal fellow who'd fallen into ruin and deep despair after the loss of his wife. The vagrant had died in his sleep and wouldn't be missed. There were more important issues to be dealt with anyway. His passing meant nothing to no one. "How sad," Thomas thought at this revelation.

The train, finally, chugged into the station from the west. A few days would pass before it returned from the east. He was anxious to move on. It seemed strange to Thomas that a menacing feeling crept into his heart. Drawing no attention to himself or to the horses in the stable down the street, he remained secluded vowing to keep his promise to his uncle. He would deliver them to the buyer far to the west.

After a time, the foreboding feeling left him, and he relaxed in the hotel. He had time to consider his next move and decided that everything would turn out right. Besides, this would be an adventure. He had been in many circumstances such as this. He hadn't had a map when he'd left his uncle David's home long ago. So why was he disappointed at this turn of events? He figured that having a name when reaching the western regions would have to be enough. He gave it no more thought.

IV

The plains spread as far as the eye could see and beyond. The landscape, however, could deceive the inexperienced. There was another river that meandered through the lowlands where cottonwoods grew and flourished. The burly countryman Thomas was looking for had crossed the vast sea from his homeland. The journey across the New World, to find a place he had dreamed of, was long and arduous. He had laid claim to a large tract of land, where he would raise a fine herd of sturdy cattle. He'd been able to somehow get his modest herd to this new country. These were not like the longhorns that were native to this area. They were shaggy beasts with kind eyes. They were hearty and resilient like the longhorns, but had a mild temperament. He kept most of his cows for a good foundation and bred his bulls to the longhorns he had acquired early in his homestead days. The crossbreeding produced a meat source that satisfied the appetites of the country.

It is peculiar that people sometimes bear similar characteristics of the animals under their stewardship. This man was of great stature, hearty, and self-reliant. With his full beard and bushy red hair, he resembled the very cattle he brought with him from his native land. He was slow tempered but determined to live life his way, giving sway to no opinion that countered his own dreams and destiny. His wife was a plump, jolly woman. With a twinkle in her green eyes, she allowed this man to be head of the house while knowing in her heart she had the last word. His children were strong and loyal to the family interests. They tended to the family business and were granted shares of the income from the cattle sales. They all shared an uncanny interest in good horseflesh—his eldest son in particular.

In his younger days Aenghas watched the herds of horses that roamed the grass plains and deserts. By the custom of the time, he would have to corral them if he wanted to claim possession of them. Some of his companions shared in his scheme. Several mares and colts were acquired over the course of two years. The mares proved difficult to break, since they had roamed free with no human contact. But the colts soon became accustomed to associating with people. Though they remained wary of strangers, this man became a familiar sight to them. He hired men who seemed to understand the nature of horses. With their help, he began developing a herd made up of the smaller native mustangs bred with larger thoroughbreds that came from east of the river. They proved a hearty lot, adapting well to the ever-changing moods of nature.

The migration of settlers from the east brought the sport of racing. In the western regions the horses were used mainly for work. There was little time to use them in games for the wagering of men. But there was always a spirit of competition between the ranchers. What games there were came to be held in the spring, as branding time rolled around. Most of the competitions involved roping skills and bronc riding. Very few horse races were held, since it seemed a waste of a good horse.

After a while, Aenghas too began to desire the clout that came with having the best and fastest horse. He sent his eldest son, Daegan, to find horses to add to the breeding program for the sole purpose of developing racehorses. Daegan's quest took him back to the east. The war was over, but still he was cautious, as he'd been instructed, unwilling to be caught up in the strife of strangers. He ventured just east of the Great River. Farther north, he found makeshift racetracks, spoke to handlers, and was sent to various farms seeking the horses that would best fit into the plans of the "Boss."

Two colts and a gray mare were found. The seller agreed that these three horses would be delivered at an appointed time. The man to deliver them would ride the mare, as it would be the only means of transportation during part of the long, challenging trip. A contract was drafted and signed. The men parted company with a handshake and flask of fine Old World whiskey to seal the deal.

V

A long shrieking blare broke the silence of a moonless night. Light in the east grew slowly, chasing the shadows into the clefts of the ground, leaving icy rime where dew had once quenched the thirst of the plains. The air was crisp, and a gusting, frigid wind hissed over the prairie grass just before the sun broke over the horizon. Being rousted so suddenly gave James the rush of adrenaline that stood him upright in an instant. His horse, also startled by the train whistle, snorted and jumped sideways. By the time the train had slowed and stopped at the water tank, he was saddled and ready to get aboard.

He helped the engineer and the scuttleman fill the train's water tank for the cooling of the great locomotive. The next settlement would be a long way ahead. Water jugs were filled for the passengers. Additional buckets were filled for the few horses and other livestock along for the ride. There was an empty livestock car that would return from the west loaded with cattle going to the packinghouses and feedlots. James chose to use it for himself and his horse so as not to draw any attention.

Looking back to the east, the three men silhouetted on the crest of the hill watching the train drew James's attention. With steam billowing from the undercarriage of the engine, and sparks flinging from the spinning wheels, the train heaved westward. Had they found his trail? That sense of foreboding again crept along his spine, giving him a shiver just as the wind cut through the cracks in the walls of the railroad car. Pulling his coat tight around him and folding his arms, he wondered what could have happened to cause their relentless pursuit.

The chill of the autumn air came as a foreshadowing of the coming winter. The almanac had predicted an unusually cold one. Huddled in the cattle car, he was sure that it would be as the almanac said. It was just September, and already it felt like late November. The train chugged on, puffing monotonously along the rails, rolling over the evenly spaced joints in rhythmic fashion.

How long he had slept, he couldn't tell, but as the train slowed to a halt, he awoke abruptly, immediately alert. With eyes wide, he peered out of the car, hoping he hadn't missed an important detail. His horse stood silent in the dark, seemingly comfortable in his stall, out of the wind and chill. Satisfied that all was well, he slid the door open to see why the engineer stopped in a desolate place. There, along the tracks, was a small wooden sign that indicated the distance to the next town. A large water tank stood high above the tracks. The engineer and the scuttleman again began to fill the water reservoir in the locomotive. Steam poured out of vents under the heavy engine, puffing and gasping as it cooled in the night air.

James got off at this stop to ride his horse the rest of the way to town. The train would travel a longer route to avoid the gullies and ravines that scarred the land. The scuttleman assured him that riding cross-country would get him to Collyre sooner than the train. Still, he hoped to bring no attention to himself and decided to take his time. As the train pulled away and the lighted passenger car passed him, he glanced into the window. What he saw made the color leave his face. He looked intently, as if peering into a mirror. He thought about the man who seemed to be looking directly at him. "Thomas," he whispered.

VI

Thurman, Reynolds, and Dobbs stood on the crest of the hill, watching the train chug out of sight. Tracking the bay stud this far, they assumed the man they pursued had boarded the train. Knowing now where the man would turn up in the next day or so, they had only to follow the tracks to Collyre. After a brief rest they rode all day and long into the night. At daybreak, they drank bitter coffee, saddled the horses, and rode steadily westward stopping at dusk by a stream. They took long drafts of the fresh water, filled the canteens and watered the horses. Then, huddled around a small campfire they talked about life with their brother who had been murdered in front of them. Their revenge would be served when the young parson was dead. From their point of view, this man deserved no mercy and would get none. The bold talk was fueled by whiskey, and the evil became more twisted with every swig from the flask.

At the first hint of war, these men had joined an ancient, elite group of sharpshooters who sold their gun-wielding skills and cowardly acts of violence to the highest bidder. Twisted minds and hellions, an ungodly lot even in their youth, craved a reputation that would strike despair into the heart of the backwoods. Each man bore a brand on his left forearm that sparked fear in everyone who had knowledge of this secret order. Its origin was traced far from the shores of the New World, where it had been cultivated in a corrupt soul guided by superstition and dark magic. They carried out their nefarious deeds without conscience or remorse, ever thirsting for blood of the next offense. Riding along the frontier assaulting remote colonies, raiding and pillaging at will, they justified their actions for their cause. The frontiersmen joined together to defend their possessions and families against these marauders known as mercenaries.

With the rising of the sun and a cold wind to rouse them, they made their way west to a gunfight of revenge. They'd been bested by a two bit gunslinger professing to be a spokesman for God, and were furious. He had not backed down from them, as they had expected, but stood his ground and won. The longer they rode, their anger and distain grew more fierce, as did their confidence and resolve, perhaps clouding their judgment.

As they neared Collyre, they stopped to sight in their guns. Their belts were full of cartridges, but they hadn't practiced for a few days. Going into this fight half-cocked could be fatal. They were no fools to be trifled with knowing the consequences of being ill prepared. Satisfied, they rode arrogantly into town making their entrance in bold fashion, sitting straight in the saddle, with one hand resting on the butt of their pistols, eyes straight ahead yet scoping the layout of the main street. Shopkeepers stopped and stared at them as they rode slowly by.

Suddenly two boys ran into the street, oblivious to the newcomers. A dog barked, spooking one of the horses, breaking the men's concentration. An inadvertent shot rang out. One of the horses began to pitch and buck, throwing the unsuspecting rider. His arm snapped when he hit the ground as his horse bolted down the street. Dobbs wailed in agony. The boys disappeared as quickly as they had entered it. Reynolds cursed the man lying in pain in the street but dismounted to help him.

"Where's the doc?" he shouted at the gawking crowd. A storekeeper pointed the way. Dobbs, accompanied by his brothers, managed to walk to the office under his own strength. This would change the plan they'd concocted during the long ride here. Still, things had to be put right. Dogging his trail, they were all the more determined to kill the parson.

The men threw the door open causing the bell to jangle loudly. They rudely clomped into the parlor, with Dobbs supporting his deformed arm. A young woman entered from the living space cordoned by a lace curtain.

"May I help?" she asked politely.

Thurman spoke with a raspy voice, impolite and demanding. "This here's Dobbs. Get the doc!"

"Let me see, now." She spoke with quiet confidence. "Please have a seat while I take a look here."

Being agitated, Reynolds drew his gun, demanding the doctor come.

She brushed the gun barrel aside and said with striking clarity, "I am the doctor. Now, have a seat in the next room so I can work. My name is Mallory Murphy."

The men stepped back in astonishment but left the room as she'd commanded. Dobbs too was skeptical and filled with distrust. Dr. Murphy took a bottle of whiskey from the shelf and offered it to her agonized patient. He looked at her intently then took two big gulps of it before handing it back. Her blond hair was drawn tightly in a bun on top of her head. Her gray eyes spoke of kindness even from behind the stern expression on her face. She was handsome, he thought.

He quickly returned his attention to his arm as she lifted it to inspect the deformity. She determined it to be broken cleanly, halfway to the elbow, making her diagnosis aloud as if she needed some approval from an invisible mentor.

"Maybe you should give me another drink before you go doin' anythin' cruel," he groaned in agony.

At that, she passed him the bottle. After he'd taken a long drink, she placed a cloth under his nose. He began to get dizzy and soon lay still. She spoke his name. Mumbling senselessly, he drifted off to sleep.

A few moments later, she emerged from the examination room to talk to the waiting men. "He will be fine," she said confidently.

Before she could give them instructions, Reynolds demanded to know when they could leave. "We got unfinished business," he snapped.

"Well, it takes time for these things to heal properly," she said slowly. "If he could stay quiet for three or four weeks, perhaps—"

Thurman swore loudly and unapologetically.

"We ain't got that kinda time!"

"Well, Mister...er...What did you say your name was?" She asked politely.

"Didn't say!" he snapped.

Beginning to feel that she was losing control of the situation, she stepped back and looked at each man. She sensed that no matter what she said, it would be wrong. Smiling, she offered them coffee instead.

"Well, at least sit a spell while your friend wakes up," she offered quietly. She went to the kitchen to fetch the coffee. Their behavior annoyed her and an uneasy feeling gnawed at her, wondering about the intentions of these men who had barged in on her. "These men are up to no good," she said.

Sensing the doctor's vulnerable predicament, the storekeeper tapped on the back door. The town was a small, close community where everyone seemed to keep a watchful eye on everyone else. He stepped quietly into the kitchen, hoping to go unnoticed by the men in the parlor.

"The sheriff is just outside, and Mr. Ballard's men are waiting on the street," he whispered. "Are you okay?"

"Yes, thank you, Mr. Morris," she answered. "But these are men looking for trouble, I fear. I best go check on my patient. Thank you." Gathering courage, she picked up a tray of coffee cups.

The storekeeper slipped away and reported to the sheriff, who stood concealed at the back door. Ballard's men were watching the front of the house, cautiously out of sight. They too had felt these men were trouble.

The doctor was precious and carefully guarded: she was the only one for nearly two hundred miles, and women doctors were extremely rare.

Her education had been very tumultuous. Her father was a generous contributor to the school of medicine, and she had graduated with honors. Being an adventurous girl, she was encouraged to explore all the possibilities in this world. She dreamed of traveling as far west as possible. At her father's bidding, the freeman who called himself Whitton Tarver, accompanied her. When the train had stopped at Collyre, the town had asked her to stay until the doctor they had hired arrived. He never came. She remained.

On this particular day, Whit had driven to a homestead to deliver dry goods. He wasn't at the house to protect her. At times like these, she had been grateful for her father's insistence that Whit should accompany her if she were going beyond the Great River.

Whit was a giant of a man, soft spoken, a trusted friend. He was a pugilist by trade but was glad to be free of the agent who had too often taken the greater share of the winnings. They had parted ways when a drunken brawl left the agent dead in an alley. Whit had come to know the Murphys by pure chance.

One night, when Miss Mallory was returning home from a late class, he had rescued her from a street gang who would have had their way with her only to leave her wallowing in filth and pestilence. He had cradled her gently and carried her home as she directed. The Murphys were ever in his debt, taking him in as if he were a beloved son returned from a victory over unknown enemies.

Dr. Murphy knew Whit would return soon, but until then she had to muster the fortitude to face these men. She took a deep breath and entered the parlor calmly, moving with graceful confidence. Not wishing to aggravate the men, she set the tray on the table. Without a word she went into the exam room surveying their faces as she shut the door. Her patient was beginning to stir. She tried to reassure him and convinced him to stay still. His arm was splinted and wrapped snuggly, but he still felt some pain. He accepted the laudanum Mallory offered and then lay still again.

Turning her eyes to the door, she stood straight, poised. Taking a deep breath, she stepped into the parlor. Speaking as one with authority, she asked them to leave their friend until the morning. The hotel down the street would accommodate their needs.

"He's our brother, and we stay here with him!" snapped Reynolds.

"I will send for you if there is any change," she continued calmly, ignoring Reynolds. She stepped to the door and opened it to see them out. Just then, Whitton came into the parlor from the kitchen, his rifle at the ready. He seemed to fill the room. The men were startled by his size and demeanor. They stepped backward and eased their posture.

"Are you all right, ma'am?" Whit asked in a booming voice.

"Yes, these gentlemen were just leaving. They will be back in the morning to fetch their friend."

The brothers gave her a long sideways glance as they stepped out the door and into the street. The sheriff and several men greeted them.

"We will have no trouble here, right?" the sheriff said firmly.

"We was just goin' to the hotel," Thurman said with his usual raspy voice. "We're not lookin' for trouble, Sheriff. Just a place to wait for Dobbs."

At that, the cowboys parted to let them pass. Reynolds scolded Thurman. "Quit tellin' everyone Dobbs's name!"

"Ah, stop worryin'. Nobody knows us this far west." He chuckled. "Just the same, I'll wire the colonel. We may need another hand."

Mallory Murphy relaxed a bit when they left. She was glad for Whit's return. She hugged his waist in relief. He wrapped an arm around her as they went to the kitchen. She found solace in the safety of his presence once again.

The sheriff watched the men enter the hotel and went directly to his office across the street. He needed to investigate this man named Dobbs. He was sure he had heard the name before.

Once in the office, Mathias Winston leafed through the telegram descriptions of men wanted by the law in neighboring territories. He pulled the wanted posters from the drawer.

Mat had come from a northern country estate some twelve years ago. He had been raised in the upper echelon of society. He and his friend Davis Edwards had been in the military together. While enlisted, they had chosen to study law as concerned with peacekeeping. When their studies had concluded, they'd found the opportunity to fulfill the burning desire for adventure and settled in the fledgling towns at the corridor to the West. He kept close to his family, though, through letters.

Finding no description to fit Dobbs, he decided to wire a lawyer friend in his hometown, after which he headed to the saloon for a draft of beer and to check on the goings-on of the strangers that frequently came and went. As he crossed the street, yet another rider passed and tipped his hat in respect for the sheriff. The rider continued down the street, and the sheriff went into the saloon.

The sun rested on the western horizon when James rode quietly into town. The shadows were long and the darkness crept into the alleys. He rode to the livery as he usually did to bed down his horse for the night. After he had rubbed down his weary mount, he went by the back way to the café he had passed. He was always wary, and he peeked through the window before entering. He chose a booth in a back corner. He would be inconspicuous there, but he'd be able see the other patrons clearly. Presently the sheriff, making his rounds, came into the café. The proprietor quickly offered the lawman coffee. Mat gladly took it and stepped toward the stranger in the back.

"So, what brings you to town?" he asked politely. "Couldn't help notice your horse. Looks a bit trail worn."

James chose his words carefully, not wishing to reveal too much about himself or his destination. It wasn't too difficult, since he had no idea where the map was to lead him. Quietly he said, "Just passin' through." Taking a sip of coffee he added, "I'll be movin' on in the morning."

The sheriff had an eye for an honest man and saw no reason to press this fellow anymore. "Rest well," he said, setting his cup on the table.

"I'd like my business to remain private," James said.

The sheriff nodded and left him alone.

The proprietor had overheard that conversation and offered James the back door. He stepped into the night and headed silently to the livery. Passing by an alleyway, he noticed three horses at the hitching rail in front of the hotel. At once he recognized them as belonging to the three men who'd been following him. That all-too-familiar feeling crept over him. Upon returning to the stable, he asked the liveryman to bed his horse in a stall not easily noticed. There was the hay shed behind the livery that could accommodate his wishes. So far, he had met only good folks here who asked few questions and eagerly offered their help.

After settling into the hotel, Thurman and Reynolds headed to the café for a meal and discuss the unfinished business with a certain "client". They knew the Parson would be packin', so they had to make sure their hand would trump his. They swore over that clumsy fool who lay at the doc's. Still, patience was necessary, and they would bide their time. The element of surprise was still on their side. Dobbs was going to be laid up for a while, however.

The proprietor filled their cups one last time and tended to the other customers. When the two left, he pondered their conversation and considered the young stranger.

At last they turned their attention to the weary horses and led them to the livery. From the security of the hay shed, James heard a commotion in the livery. Two men rustled the liveryman from his quarters to care for their weary horses. They filled the only remaining stalls. They rudely demanded that their horses be made ready to go by nine o'clock in the morning. The elderly man agreed and the brothers left for the saloon. There was a rumble of distant thunder, the first reaching arm of the impending storm. The gusting wind surged and blew tumbleweeds down the street. The tinny plinks of the piano in the saloon sang merrily late into the night.

James lay awake for a time, thinking about the man he had seen on the train. Could it really have been Thomas? If so, this might change his plans. Still, he thought, if it had been his brother, he saw no response of recognition. In spite of this inner struggle, he drifted off to sleep.

When James arose, the eastern horizon was just beginning to don a sliver of light. He saddled his horse and quietly left to camp just outside of town. Still needing some provisions before continuing, he would come back when these three scamps had moved on. James would much rather follow them for a spell just to keep an eye on their movements and intentions. He slipped away unnoticed, or so he thought.

The train whistle blared just as the sun peeked over the eastern hills. A chilled breeze blew across his face, and clouds were gathering in the west. He swore under his breath knowing it was foolish to leave a good shelter with an autumn storm on the way.

"Hell of a time for this," he said out loud. He pulled up the collar of his coat to cover his ears and pressed his hat down lower to close the gap.

The liveryman watched from the stable house. He had catered to many a stranger, but none acted so secretive and peculiar. Tuck shrugged his shoulders as he went to the tin can on the shelf and added to it the wages earned from this strange fellow. Stoking the fire against the cold, he set about making coffee before feeding his guests. Yet, looking back over his shoulder, he was curious about this fellow's behavior.

When he stepped into the stable, the horses nickered at the prospect of being fed. He brushed each one and checked for any loose shoes or sores that he could attend to. As he examined the last one, he noticed a deep scar on his chest and a number brand with a strange symbol next to it—a straight vertical line next to but separate from a diagonal slash. The number was six. "Makes no sense a'tall," he mused aloud. He thought it odd that the horse, in the corner of the stall, wouldn't make eye contact with him and seemed nervous, twitching at the thought of being touched.

The sheriff strolled in, hoping to speak with the stranger he had encountered in the café. He hadn't gotten his name and would have liked to know more about his plans. The liveryman evaded the inquiry and directed the sheriff's attention, instead, to the horse that bore the strange brand. The sheriff, curious to see for himself, entered the stall. This would change his opinion of the men at the hotel. "Dobbs," he said to himself. He had heard tell of such a brand but had waved it off as a fireside tale. Still, he would have to research this peculiar marking to further prove his theory.

At the office, he penned a letter to a teacher of the law with whom he had studied long ago. It would take a couple of weeks to get any answer. He would watch these men closely.

* * *

At the hotel, Reynolds and Thurman continued to be ill-mannered and demanding. The innkeeper tried to keep them content, hoping they would move along soon. The brothers heard the whistle blaring as the train pulled into the station. Thurman tightened his gun belt and tied the holsters down. With a swagger of superiority he pushed through the swinging door. Reynolds strapped on his heavy blade and followed Thurman, catching the door as it swung back inward, looking both directions before stepping off the boardwalk. They crossed the street and headed to the station slipping into the alley, however, to keep out of sight.

The locomotive hissed to a stop with a cloud of steam billowing from the undercarriage. A tall man, carrying a rifle, stepped from the passenger car. Scanning the platform, he strode to the stock car to check on the horses. The train would stay at the station for a couple of hours to allow the crew and the passengers a rest and a meal before heading on. It was very good business for the town. Thomas headed for the café. The proprietor directed him to the table in the back and offered a cup of coffee as if he had done so on another occasion. He told Tom of the three men looking for him.

Thomas drank his coffee quickly, thanked the proprietor for the information, and slipped out the back. How had any of these folks known about the trouble he had encountered so long ago? He wondered. Shrugging off the question, he felt compelled to be more careful until the train left. His thoughts turned to the horses on the train. He hastily went to the livery to purchase feed for them. When he entered the stable, the liveryman gasped at the man standing in front of him.

"Do you have a brother?" he asked.

Thomas answered carefully. "Yes," he whispered.

"There's three men in town a-lookin' for him. They're an angry lot intent on findin' him. It would be best if maybe you could tell him to be careful. He seems like a right fine fella, polite and all. Seems a mite strange that he would have anythin' to do with that riff-raff."

"I'm sure he has no idea what they want him for," Thomas answered quietly, recalling the quarrel between himself and the three men. He thought about the fateful meeting at the roadhouse some time back.

"I must find him!" he said with urgency. "Where has he gone?"

"Left early this morning headin' west, I believe. He didn't cotton to too many questions."

"There are two colts on the train," said Tom, pulling money from his vest. "Take care of them until I return. Keep them safe and out of sight! Tell the sheriff that these men are extremely dangerous and they are looking for me. He won't be able to handle them alone." He hurried to the back door.

"Well, who are ya?"

"Just tell him!"

Another strange fella. The liveryman shook his head again. "One of 'em has a broken arm, as I've heard tell!" he called after Tom. "He's over at the doc's now. Mr. Ballard and his boys could help out with him. Doc Murphy has Whit to help her too."

Thomas stopped and gave him a sideways glance. "The doc's a woman?" Thomas chuckled, half-amused, while he checked his gun.

"Yeah, as good as gold around these parts. But there hasn't been any rough play here before. I guess this will be a test for her skills if anythin' comes of it," he said with a worried glance down the street.

Sneaking through the corral, Thomas left the liveryman to his mumbling, making his way to the stock car at the train station. With any luck, the horses would still be standing quietly. When he reached the train, the stock door was slid open. He cautiously squatted against the wall of the station to peer under the cars along the track for any movement or shadows. He then dashed under the car. A shot rang out and a bullet splintered the wood of the stock car. Where it came from was hard to tell. Thomas had to get to the gray mare and ride hard before another shot could find its mark. He found her alert to the danger at hand. He saddled her quickly. They bailed out of the door and galloped away, ahead of a flurry of bullets. This time he had not provoked the attack.

From his place of concealment, Thurman swore as the man on the gray horse swiftly rode away. The sheriff, alerted by the gunshots, moved cautiously down the alley. He watched the rider race south from town. No one saw the shooter. He could only guess as to who fired those shots. With great haste, he made his way to the doctor's place. Maybe Dobbs would give him some insight into these events.

Mallory met him at the door. A worried look flooded her gray eyes. She hadn't been exposed to this kind of bloodshed before and had hoped to avoid it altogether.

Mat Winston insisted on speaking to the ailing Dobbs. "I must have a word with this stranger."

"He really is in no condition to speak to you right now," she insisted.

Mat persisted. "I think he has something to do with the shooting at the train station."

"He's had a lot of sedation and has not been conscious."

"Still," he said, "I must ask him before his brothers return. There seems to be a connection with the young stranger who came to town yesterday. I can't really explain it."

He entered the room where the injured man lay and found him unconscious. He was unable to rouse him. He turned abruptly to go look for his brothers.

Mallory spoke quietly, reaching for the sheriff's arm. "Be careful, Mat. These are evil men bent on killing someone. Don't give them opportunity."

He paused for a moment and gently touched her cheek. "I will be careful, Miss Murphy," he whispered.

He stepped onto the porch and checked his pistol. He holstered it and made his way to the hotel for a visit with the brothers of this injured man. He knew now that these were ruthless men. They had come from a company and time that cared not for anything but what they called the "Cause." He was no match for them, so he had to try to outwit them, make them fall into a mistake.

He faced the eastern wind, buttoning his coat. Still it cut through to his bones, and he cursed under his breath. Then he said, "I'm still livin'."

"Let's keep it that way, Sheriff," said Whit as he stepped around the corner of the house, rifle in hand.

Mat nodded to him. "Right."

Mr. Ballard's men, Mat's posse, followed the sheriff to the hotel. Whit remained to look after the doc.

Just as the men rounded the corner, they watched the two gunmen race out after the gray. The liveryman staggered from the barn and fell to the ground.

"Tuck!" Mat shouted as the men rushed to help their friend. "Tuck," he whispered, stooping over the injured man. He had been clubbed over the head and had a deep gash.

Tuck winced in pain as they helped him to his feet and escorted him to the doc's. Whit came out to help.

"Those men are weathered," Tuck muttered. "They knew you would see to me before headin' out after them. I gotta get those horses off the train before it leaves." Looking to Whit, he said, "Can you give me a hand?"

"You rest a spell. I'll get 'em," Whit said, already heading for the door.

"You know they'll be back, Mat," Ballard said as he stepped onto the front porch.

"Yeah, I know, Lou. I know. We best get a plan while there's still time. Gather your hands. I'll wire ahead and alert Davis over in Carter. He may be able to help. At least we can warn him of the trouble headin' that way." Cautiously the men stepped off the porch and headed back to the main street. Lou Ballard and his hands waited at the café while the sheriff rushed on to the telegraph office.

VII

James made his way west, intentionally staying away from the main road and the rail line. He dropped into a dry creek bed that wound along the foothills until it came to a granite wall rising high above the sandy wash. The rock-face was stained with the evidence of a forgotten waterfall. He surveyed the escarpment, searching for a way to the top of the mesa. Not far off, an abandoned trail disappeared into a crevice split apart by nature's fury.

He stepped off his horse and led him a short distance. Not knowing where the trail would lead, he tied the horse in a place of concealment and continued on foot. The trail rose steadily and at last opened up on top of the rocky plateau. It would be difficult to get his horse up the trail but not impossible. He went back to the place where he had left his horse, only to find a gray mare standing alongside the stud. She was lathered and heaving, weary from running hard and long. James rushed to the entrance of the crevice, searching for any sign of pursuit. He erased the tracks of both horses as best he could and covered the entrance with brush. After a time, he returned to the horses and led them up the trail. At first the mare balked, but with some persuasion, she followed along quietly.

Once on top of the mesa, James tethered the horses and inspected the distinct brand the mare bore on her left hip. Then he crawled to the edge of the great crag and glassed the land below. Far in the distance, the small town was now just a dot in a sea of brown and gold grassland. The puffing smoke rose and trailed behind the chugging engine that headed west, parallel to the path he'd taken. Another cloud of dust encircled what appeared to be some horsemen spurring their horses hard and fast along a southerly route.

This was a good vantage point but offered no cover. He had to find some shelter, not only from the icy wind but from the pursuit of the men who rode after him. He mounted the stud and led the mare to find a different way off the mesa and away from danger. He needed a place to think and devise a plan. Whose horse did he now have?

* * *

Thomas had raced away from town heading south. He was not yet prepared to tangle with these demented villains. He knew their breed and didn't want the town to be subjected to their violence. From what he had seen during his short stay, these people were a quiet folk, hardy but inexperienced with this kind of violence. The senseless quarrels of the nation hadn't yet reached this far west, and he hoped it wouldn't cross the Great River.

The mare was young and fast. Thomas leaned over her neck, keeping his weight off the saddle. He urged her on with his legs, giving her enough slack to gallop freely. She jumped the brush with effortless grace. The ground was a blur as she sped along. Thomas knew he couldn't ask her to keep this pace for long, but those men wouldn't be too far behind. The dry sandy soil wouldn't conceal the mare's tracks. He feared there would be no escape this time. He continued toward the mesa that rose above the desert, thinking perhaps there he could find a position in the gullies and washes to grant him some safety. He reached the mesa and drove the mare into a deep clef in the once solid stone wall. When he could ride no farther he bailed off, rifle in hand, and scrambled up the draw, clambering among the rocks. The mare, wild eyed, spun and bolted up the dry creek bed. She stepped on the rein, snapping it as she fell. She regained her footing and sped away. Thomas cursed. A cloud of dust swirled in the distance. The two men followed his trail easily and would soon find where he had dismounted. He was well armed, with his belt filled with cartridges. The rounds for his rifle were still in the saddlebags, however. He would have liked the advantage of the rifle, but relying on his aim to thwart these assassins was now the only option. The five extra cartridges he always carried in his pocket would have to be enough.

The thunder boomed ever closer and louder. Lightning burst along the clouds, lighting up the midday sky. The dark clouds moved and swirled in the gusting wind. Freezing rain began to pelt the dry ground, and the air became heavy with the smell of dampened sand. Thomas found himself gasping, as the cold wind seemed to take his breath away. He glanced around quickly, searching for better cover from the storm. He scrambled higher among the rocks.

Two sudden shots sent sparks off the granite. A ricocheting shard grazed his cheek. The sting of it made him wince and hunker closer to the ground. He slid down the slope, catching the edge of a boulder just before plunging off the ledge. Rolling quickly to a place of concealment he wiped his face with his coat sleeve smearing the blood that ran freely from the gaping wound. Lying low to the ground, he wrestled the kerchief off his neck and pressed it hard to his face. Another bullet whistled to his left, smacking the rock above his head. He pressed himself flat against the slope and sought cover away from the onslaught of gunfire.

He was on an open ledge but couldn't see where the attackers were. A way of escape eluded him. Still, he surveyed the scarp for some small crevice of refuge wherein to barricade himself and engage in the fight. Time to make a plan had passed, and he needed to find shelter now. They would be able to gain an advantageous position if he didn't act quickly.

* * *

Thurman and Reynolds followed the dust and tracks of Thomas's mare. Their horses, however, didn't have the speed nor the stamina she possessed. By the time they closed in, the horses were exhausted and would go no farther. They would have to catch him with a rifle shot. They lay in the wash and got a shot off as he scrambled up the side of the mesa. Thurman sent another shot up the slope to give Reynolds time to change position and block an escape. The wind whistled through the rocky crags. Rain filled the trenches and mud tumbled down the steep embankment. As the creek bed filled with runoff, Reynolds and Thurman looked frantically for cover, too. They clambered up the bank and moved under the boulders at the edge of the mesa. Now the odds were even. None had a horse, and all were subject to the wrath of the storm.

* * *

James moved with caution toward the sound of gunfire. He kept the horses close. They were his only chance. There was no shelter from the surging tempest that poured down on the mesa. To lose the horses now could mean losing his life. The horses reared and squealed with each clap of thunder. The lightning skipped across the granite rocks that littered the mesa. Still he moved closer to the fracas. As he reached the edge, he saw the man lying on the ledge below him. He was shifting his position among the boulders searching for the way of escape. From this vantage point, he also saw the two men in the wash begin to scurry to safety from the storm that now bore down on them. James, at last, appreciated his position on the mesa. There would be no way to help the lone man on the ledge. Doing so would mean losing the horses. He was not willing to risk that.

* * *

After a time, Thomas realized that his chance at escape had come. There had been no gunfire for a while, and he felt he must scramble to the top of the mesa. In the slippery mud, it would be a rough go, but he had to try. He took a deep breath and turned to crawl up the slope. He dug his fingers deep into the sticky clay, clawing up the side of the hill. His heels slid through the mire, but still, he was determined to reach the top and get away. Another shot and yet another ripped through his coat. Then a shot sounded above him, and he heard a cry of agony from below. He pressed upward, and with one last heaving push, he reached the top, but a boot stopped his advance. He tried to reach his gun, but before he could wield it, the butt of a rifle cut across his cheek. The wound on his face began to bleed all the more. He rolled to his back and looked up at the man standing over him. In astonishment, he cried out, "James!"

James squatted down over Thomas and chuckled as the rain pelted his face. "Did you lose your horse?" he asked with a wink. "C'mon. We gotta move away from this edge before your friends get a good bead on you. I am sorry for the blow just then. I didn't know it would be you."

They eased back across the mesa. Both men were cold, wet, and glad to finally see each other. Thomas began to weaken as they moved along. Blood stained his shirt. When he sat down, James took a closer look at his side. A bullet had struck him after passing through the Bible in his coat. They looked at each other, a bit amazed. James shrugged and smiled. It wasn't a serious wound but would need medical attention before an infection set in. He had watched his father succumb to a wound that should not have killed him. He feared the same outcome for his brother. They couldn't risk the trail that had brought him to the top of the mesa. It would lead them too close to their adversaries.

* * *

Reynolds was hit hard. Thurman was all the more determined to kill that Bible toting gunslinger. How had he gotten a shot off that hit Reynolds high in the chest? He pressed a kerchief against the wound as he pondered the direction of the shot. There must have been a second gunman above Tom Parson, he figured. That changed the whole plan. With clenched fists, he stood looking out into the veil of the storm. "You're a dead man, Parson!" he yelled. The words were empty, stifled by the pouring rain. The distant rolling thunder was the only reply. Returning his attention to his brother, he knew they had to get back to the town if Reynolds was to survive. The fight would come again.

Lightning flashed with an immediate explosion of thunder. It jolted him, and he pressed close to the rock wall. Another flash of lightning reflected off the drenched horses not far from the men. They stood quivering against the wet and cold wind under a ledge nearby. With Reynolds slumped in the saddle, they headed back to town. The rain had let up a bit, and the swelling of the stream seemed to subside. They crossed it and moved slowly. The night was long, and they eased into town just before daylight. Tying the horses in back of the doc's house, they quietly stepped into the kitchen. Shivering from shock, Reynolds stumbled to a chair as Thurman went to rouse the doctor. He was met at the parlor by Whit's rifle.

"Where's the doc?" Thurman rasped, cocking his pistol in defiance.

Just then Mallory came down the stairs, pulling her hair into a braid. "Now what?" she said firmly.

"My brother's been hit," Thurman hissed.

"Again? Whit, heat some water. Let's have a look, now." Whit gave her a puzzled glance. "Whit, please do as I ask." She followed Thurman to the kitchen.

They moved Reynolds into the small room near the parlor where Dobbs lay, still drugged, mumbling nonsense. She gently peeled his shirt back to inspect the wound more closely. She stepped back, feeling a bit faint at the sight of the gaping hole. Frothing blood seeped down his chest. The bullet had definitely hit his lung. This could become fatal if she didn't act quickly. She was determined to do all in her power to save this man, even though she sensed she would come to regret it.

Whit brought the steaming kettle and filled the basin. As he began to step to the door, Thurman turned and pressed his pistol against Whit's back. "Hold it right there! No one leaves."

The fierce flame of anger burned in the very depths of Whit's being. All reason and tolerance were replaced by a whirlwind explosion of fury. He heard the hammer lock into position. He spun around, knocking Thurman to the ground. The pistol fired into the wall above the door. With one heavy blow to Thurman's face, it was over. Whit stepped back, ready to land another, but Thurman lay still on the floor. He kicked the pistol away from Thurman's reach and dragged him out of the room.

Returning, Whit spoke softly. "Are you all right, Miss Mallory?"

"Yes, Whitton, I am now. Thank you." She paused, then sighed with relief. "Oh my, thank you. You walloped him pretty good." Rolling up her sleeves, she turned to tend to Reynolds.

VIII

"There's a flask of whiskey in the saddlebag," said Thomas. He shivered. "Don't suppose you have any dry matches?" He chuckled, then winced at the pain in his side.

James pulled the flask from the pouch. "They're worthless in this weather," he replied. "Besides, we seem to be fresh out of dry wood." With a shaking hand, he passed the flask to Thomas, who took a swallow of the whiskey, then handed it back to his brother. James put the bottle to his lips, took a swig, and stashed it in the pouch for later. He helped Thomas to his feet and steadied him as he labored to mount the mare. James led the horses across the mesa to look for a safe place to rest or an easy trail down—whichever came first.

This day had seemed an eternity, James reflected, as he trudged across the slippery mire. They came at last to the edge of the mesa on the north side. The slope seemed to be more gradual there. Easing along the rim, James found an old game trail that wound down around the mesa to the east. He left Thomas with the horses and scouted the trail before venturing ahead. After a short time, he returned, only to find Thomas lying on the ground, unconscious.

"Just great," James said aloud. After a moment, he was able to rouse Thomas again. "C'mon," he said as he heaved Thomas to his feet. "There is a good trail and shelter not too far down. We'll rest there awhile." Thomas mounted and leaned over the mare's neck as they dropped off the top into the deep shadows of juniper trees.

The night wore on. The sky drizzled, and a cold easterly wind blew. The shelter James had found was a broad cave that reached deep into the cliff. Remnants of an old fire were strewn about, the walls and ceiling charred. A fine layer of black soot covered the floor. Strange symbols and drawings were etched into the rock walls. None of them made any sense. Perhaps it was the ramblings of a shattered soul gone mad, he thought. There was room for the horses at the mouth of the cave. Weary from the day, they bent their heads low, facing away from the entrance. The wind whipped around the cave and offered little relief to the weary men. James took some jerky and cakes from the pouch and handed some to Thomas who was staring into the darkness. With his eyes glazed, he began to speak in a trance-like whisper, as if hoping no one would hear. James strained to listen and waited for the story to unfold.

"Those men are bent on killing me," he began. "They started it, and I ended it." James offered him the flask when he paused. He drew a deep breath and continued. "It has always been this way. It's the preachin' that gets me in trouble. Nobody cares about truth and justice anymore. But there's somethin' in me that won't let me stop."

James looked out into the night, recalling the arguments they'd had as young men in Grandfather's house. Those days were so long ago. Even though James didn't preach the Good Book, as Thomas had chosen to do, he had tried to live it. Every so often, when the situation called for it, he would find himself quoting scripture. But, he mused silently, he hadn't drawn a gun over the matter.

"Who are they?" James asked, still staring out into the dark. "They are ruthless, that's for sure, and obstinate." He hardened his gaze. "That town back there is not prepared to deal with the likes of them."

He contracted his eyebrows and pursed his lips. "Assassins, the scourge of humanity," Thomas said scowling. His mind cleared and his gaze softened. "But they have been careless here of late. They have been blinded by hate and greed. It may be to our advantage."

Gaining strength again, he propped himself on an elbow and laid out a plan to stop them once and for all. He meant to kill them.

"They've seen us both, but not together," he said. "Perhaps we can catch them off their guard. I believe the liveryman is the only one in that town who knows about us."

"No wonder the man in the café had seemed to recognize me," Thomas recalled. "Maybe under the cover of night, we could make it back to the livery without being seen," he said. "I think one of 'em caught a bullet, so that makes two of them left in one piece." (*He didn't know that Dobbs lay injured as well.*)

They talked long into the night, recounting the games of young boys in days of peace and prosperity on the farm, until, exhausted, they finally drifted off as sleep overtook them. The day dawned clear and cold. The ground was frozen from the rain. The gray mare nickered softly when the men began to stir. They both took a draft of whiskey and ate jerky and cake before heading out. Following the trail to the foot of the mesa they found water for the horses and some scrub grass along the creek bed. They continued to finalize their plans and started off toward Collyre.

They traveled slowly, riding in the creek bed to remain concealed. The sandy soil absorbed most of the rain, but the horses labored to slog through the bog holes that were left. In a few short days, the ground would be cracked and broken once again. They continued northeast. The livery was built close to the rail line on the southern edge of town. After riding a few miles, they turned the horses into the wind.

"I hate these easterlies!" said James. "They blow right through a man." He cursed, pulling his coat tight. Thomas grunted a response, lying low across the mare's neck.

Their shadows lengthened, and the town now in sight, they rested in a gully eroded by the countless years of flooding rains. Clouds began to gather again in the west. Thomas slid from the saddle and propped himself against the wall of the gully. There they waited for the blanket of darkness. They hoped together that the moon would rise late behind the clouds so they wouldn't be discovered.

James watched his brother, weakened from the long ride. Anguish began to stir in him. Thomas lay pale against the white sand of the gully. They had to get to the livery soon, and shelter from the cold.

IX

The town began to transform its personality as the storekeepers shuttered their windows and the sound of the tinny piano at the saloon trilled with the wind. Buckboards loaded with dry goods and families headed home. The jovial cowhands trotted their horses into town for the libations and spirits the Palace offered.

A pair of scavengers flew from the nearby rubbage pile. They squawked loudly causing James and Thomas to hunker down against the slope of the gully. With wings whirring against the wind, and shrieking calls of warning, their black shapes vanished into the darkening sky.

Night finally came upon them. James helped Thomas into the stirrup and onto the mare. He mounted the bay and moved slowly along the gully to find a shallow place to climb out. After some time, they clambered up the bank and headed to the livery just beyond the tracks. As they moved closer to town, a dog growled and barked. A light suddenly shot out of a doorway, and the silhouette of a man, rifle in hand, emerged from the house. James stopped the horses and stood in the darkness, hoping to remain undetected. The door closed, but the man lingered outside. The gray mare would give them away, James feared. Thomas, understanding the dilemma, eased the mare alongside the bay. He too hoped that she wouldn't draw attention to their position. After a time, the man opened the door and called to the dog. The sound of revelry in the saloon continued.

With a sigh of relief, James and Thomas continued toward the livery. Nearing the hay shed, James dismounted and led both horses in where Tuck had given him refuge before. The door creaked as he opened it. The horses entered gladly and snorted to clear their nostrils of dust. James eased Thomas to the ground and helped him to the cot. He covered him with the blanket and then tended to the weary horses, unsaddling them. They shook the cold from their tired bodies and munched on the loose hay that covered the floor.

Thomas spoke. "There should be two colts at the stable. I am to deliver them to Aenghas Dougan in less than a fortnight. I still have many miles to go. I was supposed to get a map from a friend of Uncle Elam to tell me where exactly to go. He was in the potter's field along the Great River. I have no map, only a name," he groaned. Then he lay still.

The map, James thought. The old man must have thought I was Thomas.

He had to get the doc. A lantern lit the ground outside the window of the liveryman's quarters. James eased the door open and crept inside. Tuck shut the door. James felt the barrel of a rifle press against his side as he turned.

"You nearly got yerself kilt," Tuck huffed. "Ever since you boys rode into town, there's been nothin' but trouble. Why, I've a mind—"

"Do you have the colts?" James asked hastily.

"Shore do," Tuck said. "Kept 'em hid jest like you asked." He paused and squinted. "Now, wait...which one are ya, anyhow?"

"I'm James. It was Thomas who asked you to keep the colts. Where are they?"

"They're in that back stall, there behind the wall." He pointed.

"Good. I need the doc. Thomas is shot up and needs more tendin' than I have skill for."

"Sounds like the doc has her hands full with that other bunch all busted up, too," said Tuck. "It'll be hard to pull her away without 'em suspectin' somethin'."

"Are there just the three of 'em?" James asked.

"Yeah, but they're a mean lot. One of 'em broke an arm fallin' off his horse when they first hit town. I heard tell Whit walloped one of 'em. Sheriff got 'im at the jail." Tuck laughed, scratching the back of his head. "They whupped me a good 'un too," he added.

"The doc's a woman?" James was puzzled.

"Ya know, she hears that a lot," Tuck said, laughing. "She's a pretty good one. This'll be a good test for her, though. Don't rightly know if she's seen this much agony before. I'll see what I can do fer ya."

"I've got him in the hay shed. Could use some grub, too, if you can." James clapped Tuck's shoulder as the liveryman turned to shuffle out.

His energy spent, James drew in a breath, mustered what strength he had left, and returned to the hay shed to check on Thomas. The bloodied shirt stuck to the wound in Thomas's side. There was no more blood oozing from the gash. He covered Thomas with horse blankets and huddled in the corner, covering himself with the hay. There they waited.

How long he had slept, he didn't know. It was still dark when the glow of the moon peeking through the clouds as they dispersed in the midnight sky illuminated the shed through the window. Thomas moaned and struggled to turn on his side, trying to ease the pain he felt.

After a while, there came the shuffle of boots to the door. James rose and quietly eased to the hinges. The door creaked open and Tuck slid in with a tray in hand.

"There's some soup Ma made up and some bread. I'll put the coffee on in my quarters," Tuck said cheerfully. He stepped to the cot. The smile was gone, replaced by a frown of grim concern. "We gotta get him someplace warm," he said. "Let's move 'im to Ma's over yonder. I'll give you a hand."

Thomas groaned as they helped him to his feet. Half dragging him, they managed to reach the boarding house beyond the corrals and the train depot. They entered the back door. James had forgotten what a warm kitchen felt like. The aroma of baked bread filled the room. He felt the sting of the night wind melt away.

Martha Parker stepped in from the parlor, pulled her shawl around her shoulders, and crossed her arms. She frowned a little as the men entered and pushed past her. Then her heart filled with compassion when she saw the injured man. She directed them to a room just down the hall from the parlor.

"Here," she said, opening the door. It creaked and they shuffled in and laid Thomas gently on the bed. James slipped his brother's boots off and gave a quick glance to Ma.

"I'll take it from here," he said. "I'll be out in a moment."

At that, Martha stepped out of the room. Shortly, Tuck returned with coffee and a slice of the fresh bread. James gratefully accepted the offerings. Thomas seemed to finally rest.

"I'll go see about gettin' the doc over here," Tuck said. He stepped out of the room.

After some time had passed, Martha tapped on the door and entered with hot water and clean cloths to bathe the wound. She had seen the devastation that comes when bullets tear the flesh and drain the body of life. She had some skills in nursing. With steady confidence she immediately began to attend to Thomas.

"Help me get this shirt off," she instructed. She carefully cut the shirt away from the wound. She brought in a flask of whiskey and offered it to Thomas before she continued. He grimaced in pain as she gently bathed the laceration. There was already redness around it but by some unexplainable luck, it had remained fairly clean.

With James's help, Thomas sat on the edge of the bed so she could bind the wound. Martha smeared a musky smelling salve along the edges of the gash and covered it with clean cloth after which she bound him with a sheet torn into strips. Thomas took another draft from the flask and lay down with a groan. Exhausted, he slept.

"Who are you fellas?" she asked.

James was reluctant to tell her, but after a moment he whispered an answer. "I'm James, and this is my brother Thomas. We've come west under different circumstances. Seems like we're meant to be together, being twins and all."

"Well, you shore have caused a ruckus, all right," she replied. "Haven't seen this much commotion since I left the plantation near fifteen years ago. Conflict has a way of steeling a person. One never seems to get used to the misery, though." She cleared her throat and swatted at some unseen image in her mind. "Enough of this nonsense," she said, scolding herself.

Returning her full attention to Thomas, she wiped his brow gently, whispering in a language that James hadn't heard before. Her melodic words flowed from her lips with the enchanting eloquence of a southern mistress. Thomas mumbled a response and fell silent cloaked in a dreamless sleep.

James sipped on the coffee. It had a musty aroma and sweet flavor. He felt a warmth creep into his muscles, and peace flooded his soul.

Ma Parker left the room, only to return a short time later with a bowl of steaming water. To it she added some leaves and crushed berries. She crumbled dried flowers over the mixture. A sweet fragrance filled the room. James felt the tension leave him and noticed that Thomas seemed to breathe easier.

Ma Parker spoke softly, only a passing thought. "Lavender quiets the soul."

James relaxed, closed his eyes, and faded into unconsciousness.

She turned the lamp low and left quietly, locking the door behind her. In the fireplace, the flames leapt and crackled merrily. To unsung music, the shadows danced among the furniture of the small room. Nothing disturbed the brothers' slumber.

X

Thurman groaned and rubbed his face to clear his head. He got up and began to rattle around the jail cell. "Hey!" he shouted. Then he repeated himself, louder.

"Shut up!" yelled an unseen man.

The door to the office slammed shut leaving him in the dark. A chill filled the cell. He looked out the window, hate consuming him. He seized the bars and shook at them, cursing the very existence of this worthless town. His muscles tense with rage and exasperation, he bellowed until the piano player at the Palace paused. A hush came over the whole town. Shrouded by the night, the scavengers took flight. The beating of their wings faded away in the dark. Then, the prairie was silent. The saloon slowly emptied as would-be revelers felt a shift of moods. The sound of horses trotting away echoed in the deserted street.

Dobbs shot up in bed and reached for a pistol that wasn't at his hip. He was jarred back to reality as the pain in his arm caused him to scowl and moan. It throbbed. He cursed and reached for the flask left on the night table. Taking three swigs, he groaned and lay back, shifting his arm to a position of some comfort. Whit opened the door and glared at him.

"Don't you wake Miss Mallory! She's much nicer than I am. I don't cotton to yer yelpin'. You jest mind yer manners, ya hear!" He shut the door. Dobbs heard the turn of the key and the creak of the wood floor. He looked around and found no windows. The only way out was through that door, and beyond it was a man bent on seeing to it that no one came in or out. He heard the creak of the rocking chair. There was no escape.

Reynolds snorted. Dobbs looked over at him, perplexed at this unexpected situation. What had happened, he couldn't tell. He wondered at the fate of Thurman. He was troubled and listless throughout the night.

The door opened after some time, and Mallory entered carrying a tray. The aroma of coffee immediately filled the room. Reynolds stirred, and Dobbs squinted at the light that seemed to flood the otherwise darkened room.

"What's the time?" Dobbs asked. Sitting up and swinging his legs off the side of the bed, he ran his fingers through his greasy hair.

"It is seven o'clock," Mallory answered abruptly, setting the tray on the table. "It's morning. I've brought some breakfast for you. Has Reynolds woken at all?"

"He moans now and again," said Dobbs. "What happened?" Then it came to him. "How do you know his name?"

"All I know is they came barging in the other morning. He had been shot in the shoulder. I think his lung is compromised as well."

She proceeded to tend to Reynolds. His breathing was labored. She frowned as she clipped the dressing to inspect the wound. There was nothing she could do about the fever he had. She knew that there was infection setting in and feared the man might lose this battle. Dejected, she turned away. What more could she do?

With a sense of resolve she spoke. "Ma Parker could help. Whit, go to Ma's and have her come quickly if she will."

Whit hesitated.

"Please?" she asked.

He nodded and hurried out the door.

Whit stopped in at the sheriff's office. The deputy sat at the desk with his feet propped up. When Whit entered, the lawman sprang to his feet, rifle in hand.

"Hey, you gave me a start there, Whit."

"Where is Master Winston?" Whit asked. "I need fer someone to go stay with Miss Mallory. Those two coyotes are down at her place, and I jest don't trust 'em, even if they are busted up. I gotta go fetch Ma on accounts that feller ain't doin' so good. Miss Mallory has done all she can, but she jest don't want to lose 'im."

"Well, I believe he's over at the Palace with Mr. Ballard and his hands," he said. "They're tryin' to figure what to do with those galoots. Maybe one of them would oblige. I gotta keep an eye on this one." He nodded toward the door.

"Yeah," Whit snorted. He stepped to the door and pounded his fist. "Jest you behave!" he yelled. "Next time you'll need a hole dug." He gave a wink to the deputy. "That should do it." He chuckled and headed to the saloon.

Mat Winston and Lou Ballard sat at one of the poker tables with the foreman and two other hands. Whit stepped to the table and asked if one of the them would go stay with the doctor. Clayton Knox volunteered and left quickly. Whit walked out with him.

"Thanks," he said, raising his rifle. "I'll be back with Ma pretty soon." They parted, each going about his own task.

At the gate, a sign swung freely in the breeze: **Parker's Boarding House**. Whit entered the yard and stepped up onto the porch. A steel-gray calico cat yowled and hopped onto the railing.

Before he could ring the bell, Ma opened the door and greeted him. "Did Miss Mallory send ya? Come in, Whit. I've got what she'll be a-needin'," she said, before Whit could say hello. "These leaves will work best if she boils the water before addin' 'em. Prayin' wouldn't hurt neither."

With the herbs and leaves Whit stepped outside. He turned and looked into Ma's black eyes, the unfathomed abyss to her soul. He shuddered before speaking. "She had hoped you'd come."

"Nah, not yet. She's always tryin' to save the snake." She pointed a finger at some invisible phantom. "Won't come to nothin'. He'd a-soon bite cha as not. She needs to make a poultice and bind it tight. That lung'll be sick for a long time. Maybe never heal!" She hollered when Whit passed into the street. "I come if'n she really needs. You know that, Whit. You tell her, y'hear!"

Whit walked on. "How'd she know it was a lung?" he said out loud. Shaking his head, he hurried back to Dr. Murphy.

Ma went back into the house and closed the door without a sound. She prepared the coffee and went to the room where the brothers stayed. The strong aroma that filled the room caused them to stir.

James sat up in the chair and rubbed the sleep from his face. Stretching, he rose to take the tray that Ma carried in with her.

She checked the dressing on Thomas's side. He winced as she pulled on the bandage.

"Looks a mite better, today," she said. "Seems Miss Mallory is tendin' the fellas that followed ya here." She placed a fresh poultice and bandage over the gash. "Lucky you brought him when you did. He might not be here now." She gave Thomas a draft of a bitter drink. He wrinkled his nose in protest but managed to take a couple of swigs. It felt warm going down.

"He'll eat later today," she reassured James. "He jest needs to sleep now, and give that poultice a chance to work its magic." She winked and offered James a cup of coffee.

"So what was in the coffee last night?" he asked.

"Ah, something to carry away yer troubles. Perhaps they will return, but yer safe here for now. Do not look out the window while you are here. Trust me, now."

"Thomas has unfinished business farther west. He's got horses at the livery that—"

"It'll keep," she snapped. "You rest and get strong again." Then she lowered her voice. "That journey will have troubles of its own." She stepped to the door. Without turning, she said, "Tuck takes care of them." At that she closed the door, and James heard the key turn in the lock.

Thomas was again resting peacefully, breathing deep and steady. James sat at the table and ate what Ma had meticulously prepared. The coffee was refreshing and strong. He felt good again. He considered the circumstances that had led to this unfortunate twist of fate. His thoughts and memories seemed to be clear. Vivid images of his childhood filled his mind as if it were yesterday. He reflected on those years of youth and the good times they'd had on the farm so long ago. He found himself talking to his brother as he slept. Even in slumber, shifting in his dreams, Thomas mumbled a response, with a wrinkled brow or mischievous grin.

Behind the locked door, James didn't feel imprisoned. Yet he sensed, for the first time, someone else had his back. It felt odd to be trusting in folks who were strangers and yet friends somehow.

Later in the day, Thomas awoke clear minded and ready to eat, just as Ma had predicted. He sat up in bed and looked at his unfamiliar surroundings. James stood near the window. He didn't lift the sash but stood silently, staring at the curtain. When Thomas stirred he turned and left his thoughts suspended in oblivion.

"How are you feelin'?" he asked, stepping to the bed.

"Not too bad, actually," Thomas said. "How long has it been?"

"Three days since you took that bullet. Ma has some kinda magic stuff she's been usin'. The herbs and leaves she brings is different than any doctorin' I've heard tell of. It doesn't matter as long as it works, right?"

"So, where's the doc? Why didn't you get her?" Thomas asked.

"The doctor's a woman," James echoed. He paused in thought for a moment before continuing. "Seems she's carin' for those other fellers who are after me, or...Why are they after you, anyway? I've never seen them before, so they must think I'm you."

Thomas mustered a grin at all the questions James was posing. "If you'll let me explain...You may want to sit down, there." He gestured to the chair by the bed. James folded his arms and gave a sigh of irritation.

He told James of all that had befallen him after his hasty departure from the pulpit where Grandfather had preached, leaving very little to the imagination. It was as if he was confessing his sins and baring his soul to resolve the guilt he had carried with him these many years. He felt relief and a burden lifted from him as he continued his story.

James pulled the map from his vest pocket and handed it to Thomas. He inspected it and smiled as he gave it back to James. It was just as Uncle Elam had said.

The room began to dim as the sun inched to the west. Ma knocked gently on the door, opened it, carrying two plates of supper.

Thomas smiled and said, "I am pretty hungry, come to think of it."

"Smells good," added James.

Ma set the tray on the table and gestured to Thomas. "Now you come sit right here. These here vittles will set real good on your stomach. Don't eat too fast. Go easy now. Come now, eat up. You'll be a-needin' your strength if'n you plan to travel soon."

"When is the train due back from the east?" James asked. "We really need to get goin'. Besides, I'm sure you folks would like us to take our troubles elsewhere."

"You mean them fellas down yonder there." Ma nodded toward the doctor's house. She turned with her eyes fixed on the fireplace. The flames danced and crackled brighter. She threw a powder into the flames. They hissed and flared with green smoke. She began to speak as if in a trance. "They will come after you. You must be alert and ready. There is open country beyond the mesa. You mustn't let them catch you there. The horses will slow you down. Ride the train for a day and then get off after it crosses the ravine. There is shelter there in Bullrim. You must find a trail that winds into the canyon. It is steep and rocky, but that will be best for you. The trail will bring you to a valley lush and green, with many tall pine trees." She took a deep breath and closed her eyes. With a smile on her face, she whispered, "Can you smell them?" Opening her eyes again, she turned to James. "It will be best if you go alone. Thomas will follow. Give him the map."

Her posture eased, but the burden of her words seemed to rob her of strength. "Eat. There is much yet to do." She stepped out the door but didn't lock it. From beyond the door came a muffled response. "The train will be here at six o'clock tomorrow morning.

We'll get word to the engineer to watch for you at the water tank. Be ready."

James and Thomas looked at each other. "Have you ever heard such a thing as that?" James asked. "And how did she know about the map?"

"You know, there was talk about women in the swamps farther south that seemed to have a gift of seein' things and knowin' things. I just never saw it for myself till now. I always thought it was a yarn. Kinda gives a man the creeps." Thomas shuddered as he spoke.

They decided that Thomas was to ride the bay stud while James would ride the gray mare and take the others. Thomas gave him the papers. James slipped them into his vest pocket and handed the map to Thomas. No one could know their plans other than Ma, not even Tuck, though he would figure it out for himself. Thomas would wait until his adversaries left before following James. Neither of them knew how this would play out. Ma had not offered any knowledge of the outcome. They talked well into the night. The only light in the room was from the fireplace. They took care to stay away from the window so as to cast no shadow on the blinds that would give them away.

It was still dark when Ma quietly entered the room. As she spoke, James felt strength come upon him, and he woke alert, rejuvenated, and eager to be on his way. "Come, it is time. Tuck has prepared the horses. They are rested. The gray is magnificent. She is wise and kind. She will bear you to your destination. Great will be her off-spring. Keep the North Star in your right hand. Travel by night as best you can. Trust the mare."

She had with her a bedroll of thick wool. In the pouches of the saddlebags were fresh cakes and jerky. There was also a flask.

"Drink from it when you are weary. It will warm your soul and give you strength," she said, sensing James's thoughts.

He shook his head in bewilderment. Thomas took the Bible from his coat pocket and handed it to James. The ripped pages would remind him of the evil pursuing him. They exchanged pistols to make the illusion complete. They shook hands, and each clasped the other's shoulder. Without a word, James nodded and slipped out the door.

Ma followed him to the kitchen. Extinguishing the lamp, he stepped out into the darkness. Then he turned to her and whispered, "Why do you help us?"

"Go," she said. "Soon you will know."

James jogged to the stable, keeping low in the shadows of the fences and buildings. When he reached the hay shed, the bay stud nickered softly to him. He stroked his face and whispered, "Not this time, fella. Settle down, now." The great horse fidgeted and stamped his feet. James hurried to the gray mare. Tuck had her saddled and tied the others to the hitch rail by the forge.

"Well, er, Thomas," he began. "Looks like that gash is a mite better now, eh?"

"Yeah," James answered, trying to act the part.

Tuck scratched his thinning hair and adjusted his hat. He pressed his fingers into James's chest. "You do as Ma says, and you jest may live through this. Make one mistake, and it'll cost ya—maybe everything. I'll see to it yer brother follows soon. You'll be a-needin 'im, I reckon."

James knew these two people would keep their secret. He felt better leaving Thomas with them. Still, he was curious about their foresight.

"The train will take on water a couple miles up the tracks. Follow the gullies. Those fellas ain't goin' nowhere for a while at least. It should be safe, but stay low anyhow. No one knows there's two of ya. And no one will if'n we can keep you apart. Go on, now, Tom," he whispered, swinging the door shut. It creaked, and James heard the crossbar settle into place.

James was an honest man. He felt it strange to be cast as an imposter but he had chosen to fill his brother's boots, taking his name for a little while. He mounted the mare and headed to the wash beyond the tracks. The sandy soil buffered the sound of the mare's foot falls. A stiff wind blew across his face. Sand whipped around the horses. The tracks they left seemed to magically disappear. The eastern horizon began to take shape as dawn approached. James quickened the pace when he heard the whistle blow. The train would stop for an hour or so while supplies and mail were exchanged. He was sure that Tuck had arranged his boarding at the water tank.

As James trotted the mare through the wash, the light of the new day winked over the horizon. The water tank stood just a short distance away. He decided to hole up a ways off. If he could approach the train and ease alongside it, maybe he could get to the stock car unseen by any of the other passengers.

He dismounted a few hundred yards from the track just west of the tank to wait. He felt the presence of evil that seemed to be closing in on him. Staring off to the east, he heard a voice in his head. "Malevolence has come to consume you. Do not be overcome." He shivered and then heard the long blare of the whistle. Had he fallen asleep? How had the train come up to the tank so quickly? Nearly two hours had passed, as far as he could figure by looking at the position of the sun.

The engine sat gasping and puffing, steam pouring out from under it. The engineer and scuttleman were busy with the task of filling the boiler in the belly of the locomotive. The engineer stepped to the front of the train when he saw James with the horses approaching.

"Tuck told me to meet you here," James said.

"Yup," the engineer replied. "Ever'thin's set, so git on up there in the stock car. There's a duffel that Ma gathered for ya." He rubbed his chin and looked out of a half-closed eye. "Don't make much sense, though. Ma don't take to strange folk. She meant to put a curse on me if'n I don't take real good care of ya." He looked up and down the tracks as he climbed into the cab of the locomotive.

James led the horses along the train. Nearing the stock car he heard the door slide open, and a ramp was pushed out on an embankment along the tracks. The horses followed him in. There were stalls for each of them filled with feed and straw.

"Hi," a boy said cheerfully. "I'm Dude—er, Dudley." He offered his hand in greeting.

James returned the gesture. "I'm pleased to know you, Dude."

"Tuck told me to be ready for ya," he said as he led the gray mare to a stall. James followed with the colts. "I took this job last summer. I just ride as far as Carter, watching out for the livestock that gets shipped here to there. Mom cooks stuff for the café. Betcha ate her chicken there once. She's the best cook in the county. Everyone says so."

Without further delay, the train lurched forward. The couplings clanked, each in turn, from the power of the engine. The sound rumbled as if it were an echo bouncing on the walls of a deep chasm. Sitting together with a cake that his mother had made for him, they ate while Dude recounted his childhood adventures and dreams for a better future. James listened intently, smiling and nodding while Dude spoke, reminiscent of his own life's story. They chatted casually. Dude described the unexplainable mystique of nature's formations in the land where James planned to go, expressing his genuine love for the incomprehensible beauty that surrounded them.

"God exists. The evidence is everywhere. How can anyone deny it?" he finally concluded.

Looking down he muttered, "Pa got real sick and died last year. Doc Murphy couldn't save him. She was so sad, but she worked night and day to make him better. Ms. Parker couldn't even get him well. Anyways, I jest had to get a job to help out. Mom wants me to learn my letters and numbers. I try to do that when I'm ridin' along. She helps me some when I get home."

James thought about his grandmother's instructions. He missed her but didn't take any stock in grieving anymore.

"Ma Parker told me to get off after we crossed the ravine," James said, changing the subject. "How far is that, exactly? I would like to be ready."

"Ah, it's about forty miles or so. Never really measured it," Dude said. "Takes a few hours, I reckon."

"Any strangers get off the train back in town?" James asked.

"There's always strangers comin' and goin'," Dude said. "There was a couple of fellas that didn't get back on the train. One was a preachin' man, I think. The other was a tall, well-dressed feller. He had a dandy walking stick. Both of them were pretty well armed. Not the cowhand type, if ya know what I mean."

James shifted his thoughts to Thomas. The town would protect his identity, he was sure of it. He had to believe in the people he had met there. At any rate, there wasn't anything he could do to help Thomas. Besides, he *was* helping by pretending to be him. He had to trust his brother as well as his new friends in Collyre. Still, he puffed and chewed on the end of his pipe searching for a clear resolution to this deranged, unfettered evil bent on his annihilation. The train clacked along the rails with no regard for this inner strife that vexed James.

XI

An hour passed since James had left the livery with his horses. Thomas regretted sending him off on a mission that had him openly pursued by evil men who were intent on assassination. James had done nothing to deserve that fate.

"Still, I'm in no shape to travel so far," Thomas mumbled.

The eastern horizon began to glow a pale orange. He heard the long blare of the whistle. Looking at the clock on the mantle, he said, "The train is late."

Ma Parker entered the room with coffee. "Your brother got off and should be well on his way to meet the train at the water tank. You must stay here for a time," she said quietly. "I am afraid for you and your brother. The one that is coming will command the men who mean to inflict grievous harm upon you and your brother. I hope that I am wrong, but I have a very heavy heart whenever he is close by."

"Who is it you fear?" Tom asked, sensing her anguish. "You can't disguise the dread in your voice."

"The colonel is an evil man invading my life once again. He slaughtered my family and would kill me too, if only he knew I was here." Her lips quavered as she stared into Tom's eyes.

It was Tom who broke her gaze. He felt an uneasiness drift into his heart, the fingers of a gripping shadow creeping into an empty room choking the clarity of resolute thought.

Thomas leaned forward on the bed and looked deep into Ma Parker's black eyes. "I will help you overcome this madness," he heard himself say. He reached for a cup, his gaze still fixed upon her eyes.

Ma touched his hand. Trembling, she whispered, "It will be dangerous. I must warn you before you commit to this insanity. The way before you is beyond my vision, and I cannot foretell your portion. Do not doubt yourself nor your brother, no matter what is brought to light. I know in my heart you are a good man, but I fear you will have to prove yourself. There is nothing this man, this parasite, wouldn't do to crush your very soul."

They sat in silence, each trying to plan the next move. After a time, Martha Parker stood and spoke with resolve. "I will call for Tuck, and we will lay open a plan as best we can. No one but Tuck and I have seen both of you together. It could work in our favor. Perhaps we could convince these tramps that you have moved on. It could buy some time for your brother to outrun them, at least for a while. They will ultimately pursue him, thinking all the while it is you they follow. I fear for Miss Mallory. She is innocent and not ready for this infestation. I cannot face the colonel yet. My destiny is dark before me. I will go to the mesa and wait for a time. There is a cave near the top. My spirit will counsel you. You will hear my voice in the whispers of the night wind. I will speak to you in dreams. Look to the skies. The scavengers will guide you. I will ask Miss Mallory to care for you in my absence."

As she fell silent, Tuck tapped on the door. "Ma, that colonel fella is coming," he whispered. "I took the sign down."

Opening the door, Ma waved Tuck inside. She adjusted the shades and turned the lamps low. She put leaves and berries in the kettle that hung over the flames in the fireplace. Soon an aroma filled the room. It smelled musty but cleared their minds. Thomas thought he had smelled these herbs before but couldn't recall when.

It would be difficult now to get word to Miss Mallory without being seen. Even Tuck's presence would give Ma Parker away.

"We must shutter the windows quickly, before it gets light," said Ma. "It may be that he won't take notice of it." She doused the fire. Tuck went out the back and to the livery. Somehow, they had to get word to Miss Mallory about Thomas. He still needed some attention. He was at least well enough to hide in the shed of the livery again. Ma gathered a basket of bread and herbs. Wrapped in heavy robes, she quickly headed for the mesa.

Everything was moving too quickly, Thomas thought. He hurried to the shed hoping no one would see. He heard Tuck rattling around in his quarters, emerging, he carried a rifle and ammunition. Thomas opened the door for him.

"No time to explain," Tuck said, seeing the question in Thomas's eyes. "The stud is in the back stall. They may not find him right away. I'm hopin' to get word to the sheriff that you've gone. I don't know what you've done or why they're after ya, but you best be tryn' to get outta here soon. I was hopin' to give your brother a better head start. I jest don't know now." He shook his head. "I'm gonna try to get to Miss Mallory. You stay put."

He stepped out and looked around cautiously before heading out into the desert. There was still some cover of darkness, but announcing the coming dawn, a rooster crowed. Tuck jumped the tracks and made his way alongside the train, making sure not to be seen from the passenger car. Just as he passed it, a tall man with a heavy walking stick stepped down to the platform. Tuck pressed himself against the mail car. Crouching down, he looked under the car and grimaced. It was the colonel, just as they had feared. A man spoke, and the colonel turned to acknowledge him. They spoke in hushed tones, the words lost to the chuffing of the train. Two other fellows got off briefly. After a muffled conversation, they boarded once again. Two horses were unloaded from the stock car. The colonel and the man gathered their possessions and with the horses headed toward the hotel. Tuck watched from his position of concealment before heading over to Miss Mallory's place.

Tuck reached the back door. Hearing voices inside, he crept to a window, and saw Whit and Clayton. He tapped on the window to get their attention. Whit looked out, and saw that it was Tuck. With his rifle in his hand, he came to the door and gestured for Tuck to step in. Declining the offer, he quickly relayed the message that the stranger had moved on, if anyone were to ask about him. He handed a letter to Whit that was addressed to Miss Mallory.

Before hurrying away, he turned to Whit. "Don't mention Ma Parker nor myself," he commanded. "There's a couple of fellas that just got off the train that we'd just a'soon not know our whereabouts." With that, he ran out into the desert.

Whit watched his friend run off before returning to the kitchen. He chuckled as he poured coffee for Clayton.

"That old coot," he said with a smile. "He's done some pretty strange stuff, but if that don't beat all. He said somethin' about a stranger movin' on. Do you have any idea what he's talkin' about?"

"Sheriff was talkin' to a stranger in the café the other evenin', about a week ago, I reckon. Never did get a good look at him, though," Clayton said. "I'll make mention of it next time I see Mat. See ya later, Whit. Thanks for the coffee." He headed out the door.

* * *

The colonel and the reverend settled into rooms overlooking Main Street. The colonel chose the corner room, with windows on the south and west-facing walls. He had a clear view of the train tracks and Main Street. They went to the café for breakfast. They sauntered in, pausing at the door long enough to survey the patrons.

A couple of cowhands were engaged in casual conversation with the proprietor, and a woman pouring coffee greeted the guests. Choosing the table in the back, the colonel positioned himself to watch the door.

Soon Clayton walked in and joined the cowboys from the LV Bar B. He glanced at the men in the back but paid them no mind. He sat down with his back to them and spoke quietly to his friends. Finishing the last of their coffee, they left quickly and headed to the sheriff's office. The colonel watched them, trying to speculate the actions of these cowhands.

The reverend fidgeted, but the colonel calmly returned his attention to eating. After savoring the breakfast, he and the reverend stepped out onto the boardwalk. Surveying the main street, they, too, ventured to the sheriff's office. As they rounded the corner, the cowhands mounted their horses and headed in an easterly direction out of town. Mat Winston was standing on the porch of the office when the colonel and the reverend greeted him.

"I am Colonel Dosiere from the eastern territories," he said, offering his hand in a gesture of respect. "I have gotten word from my deputies that a vile man is near to these parts. I have a warrant for his arrest and a poster. He claims to be a preachin' man but is nothing but a thief and murderer. He's known as Parson. Don't rightly know his given name."

The sheriff pondered this description and thought about the man leaving town hastily on the gray. He looked at the poster and at once recognized the young fellow he had spoken to earlier in the week. He revealed nothing to the colonel but said a young man looking similar had come and then gone, but didn't say which direction he rode. He hadn't been aware of any warrant for the man.

Thurman overheard the conversation and began shouting to be released. The colonel, recognizing the voice, brushed by the sheriff and stepped toward the cell. The sheriff quickly stepped in front of him. The colonel stopped abruptly and rapped the walking stick on the floor. "You, sir, are holding my deputy, a lawman such as yourself. If ever we are to catch this rogue, you must release him!"

"Lawman or no, he threatened our doctor. We will not tolerate it!" Mat snapped, standing firm.

The reverend widened his stance and reached for his gun. The colonel eased his demeanor. The reverend let the gun slide back into the holster and stepped back.

"Your cooperation is imperative in capturing this elusive fellow," the colonel said in a softer tone. "He killed a deputy east of here, beyond the Great River. My men have followed him thus far."

"As I said, he has moved on. This is a small town, Colonel," said Mat. "Had I known about this man I would have had him in my jail instead of this guy. You may want to check over at the doc's. I believe his brothers are there, a bit busted up. One of them is shot, and the other has a broken arm. Looks like you're a mite short on deputies."

The colonel chuckled at the irony but bid the sheriff good day. Stepping into the street, he turned to Mat. "Which way to the doctor?"

The sheriff nodded his head to the right and added, "Just on the edge of town, the white house and picket fence."

Mat didn't like either of these men. He was a good judge of character most of the time. What the colonel had said made no sense, but he decided to play along for a while. He believed that if one is patient, the truth always has a way of revealing itself in due time. Still, he wondered where the young stranger had gone. He'd not given any thought to him since their brief meeting in the café a while back. Then he thought, "That young fella rode a dark bay, didn't he? Then who was on the gray? There are no other strangers in town. If that was him, where'd he get the gray? Where's the bay?" The riddle annoyed him. As he shut the office door and locked it, he heard Thurman protest again. He shook his head and walked up the street.

XII

Aenghas looked at his watch as he stepped out onto the porch. It would be sunrise soon. The horizon was beginning to pale, and the stars, that had been twinkling brightly in the crisp fall air, were extinguishing, fading into the expanding brilliance of the sunrise. Even the distinct pattern of Orion in the southern sky would eventually surrender to the greater light. This was his favorite time of the day. The birds had not yet been roused. Silence and peace filled his mind, allowing deeper thoughts to shape the character of his soul. From his homeland he had brought with him a Bible, written in the old language of his ancestors. When times were hard it brought solace and encouragement to persevere in this harsh, unforgiving wilderness.

The time had passed that was agreed upon for delivery of the three horses. He couldn't bring himself to believe that the men Daegan had dealt with would deceive him. There had to be another explanation. What could have gone wrong? He would give the man one more day and then send telegrams of inquiry to the towns along the way. Perhaps someone would have information pertaining to the whereabouts of the man who'd promised to deliver the horses. He would have to stop at the liveries, Aenghas thought, to rest the horses. Even riding the train would be tiring for both the rider and horses.

Just before the sun burst over the horizon, a brisk wind swirled around the porch. The chimes rang as the pipes jingled and swung freely. The rooster crowed and strutted from the barn. The hens in the coop began to cackle and cluck, ready for the morning feed.

Daidre opened the door and offered her father a steaming cup of coffee. He had smelled it even from beyond the closed door. She pulled her coat tight and held it while she sipped her own coffee. Winter would soon be upon them, but they were well prepared. Wood was chopped and piled on the porch. The hay was put up in the shed, protected from the elements. It had been a good crop this year.

There were several farms along Bullrim River, but there was always water aplenty. Aenghas had built the homestead long before the others had arrived, so he had the most water rights, but he was not a greedy man. He shared what he had with neighbors in need. He always felt that good deeds would spur close friendships and hoped for the same respect he showed to others. He taught his children to behave likewise.

The Bullrim flowed out of the north. No one knew its source because of the rugged canyon through which it flowed. The churning rapids in the gorge were unforgiving. When the railroad had come, many men perished on the granite boulders while building the trestle spanning the deep gorge. Some say the rocks groaned and shifted in the night, leaving the trusses unstable. At last the railroad company prevailed. The engineers lauded it as a masterpiece. Few, however, dared to ride the train across that span. Beyond the gorge the river flowed quietly through the meadows, the water was ice cold and sweet to the taste. It meandered through the pastures where the grass along the bank was lush and always green. The mushrooms popped up in rings among the giant cottonwoods that flourished just west of the ranch house. The smell of damp soil filled the early morning air and fog drifted over the low-lying fens to the south. Yes, at this hour of the day, Aenghas was content.

He decided to ride to town and check the train's arrival schedule. He had heard a distant whistle a week or so ago. The train should be just about due to come again from the east.

Daegan and some of the other ranchers were gathering cattle before the weather turned bitter. There would be some back riding to do, but they would bring the majority by week's end. Every year they sorted and drove the herds to their respective pastures. Come spring, they would gather together again and help with the branding.

His sons would be there to watch over things while Aenghas and Daidre rode to town. They prepared to leave the next morning at first light for a full day's ride. They put together provisions and would stay with family in town.

Graeme rose early and hitched the team. Ailene gave them a list of goods she would need. She had packed some cake and jam, a bit of coffee, and pickled beef for them. Blankets were carefully laid in a trunk under the seat. "Just in case," she said. The brisk wind swirled around the porch, the chimes tinkling as they set out. The bright sun peeked over the horizon—the promise of a new day.

Aenghas drove the team. He always made an excuse so Daidre could ride a horse. From the time she was small, she had ridden. She cried at the very thought of being stuck in the wagon. The times she rode in front of Aenghas, she would fall asleep to the melodic clip-clops and rhythmic sway of her father's horse.

The day began clear and cool, but there was the distinct smell of rain on the breeze. As the morning passed to noon, the clouds began to gather in the west. They were but halfway to town when the first raindrops dampened the road before them. In the distance the dark gray clouds were lit with instantaneous flares of lightning, after which the thunder rumbled deep and menacing. The wind began to blow more fiercely now. Daidre buttoned her tunic, yet her hair was blown in every direction. Aenghas hurried the horses to a stand of trees near a granite boulder to find shelter for the duration of the storm.

He drove the team along the rock wall out of the wind. There he opened the tarp. Daidre tied her horse to the wagon while Aenghas held the driving lines of the team. He had fixed the brakes of the wagon to keep the horses from bolting at the piercing flashes of lightning and explosive claps of thunder. The horses stood quiet, glad to be out of the storm's fury.

Aenghas turned his thoughts to Daegan, knowing he and the cowboys with him would have to find shelter from the storm. Perhaps they were far enough to the north and beyond the fingers of wrath that now bent down on them.

* * *

Ailene stood on the porch of the ranch house, wrapped in her shawl, looking both north and west. Her family was beyond her reach. She picked up the Bible and sat waiting in silent prayer and constant vigil. Graeme, understanding her distress, kept the fire stoked and the coffee hot. As the day lengthened, the rain poured down upon the ranch so that she couldn't see beyond the fence around the yard. The Bullrim overflowed its banks, flooding the yard halfway to the porch. Still, she waited, watching from the window of the parlor.

Graeme went about his chores after his father and sister left for town. The storm kept him inside most of the day, though he managed to clean the barn and spread dry straw in the stalls. He hurried across the yard to the porch, brushing the water from his coat before he opened the door to the kitchen. The sweet smell of spice cake and coffee greeted him as he stepped in.

"I'll go to the east pasture and check on the horses when the storm passes," he said to his mother as he sliced the cake. She set a cup of milk on the table and handed him a fork.

"This looks to stay awhile, Graeme," Ailene spoke softly. "Can't it wait until Daegan gets home?"

"I'll wait till this afternoon," he answered. "Daegan should be home by then."

At last, the rain subsided, and as the sun set, the clouds began to break, allowing the last beams of day to kiss the saturated fields with a crimson glow. Ailene was glad Graeme had stayed with her.

"Red sky at night, shepherd's delight," she murmured. It was an old saying from beyond the sea that she had learned growing up a farmer's daughter.

Daegan and the hands rode into the ranch after it had gotten dark. The cattle were left in the northern pasture, away from the floodwaters of the Bullrim. They had indeed missed the full measure of the storm but were glad to be home. Ailene was relieved to have her son and his friends home safe. She would rest easier now.

Graeme helped his brother settle the horses in the barn. He had pitched hay into the mangers earlier. Ailene had prepared supper for them and served the weary men. They recounted the gathering and told Ailene of the adventures of young men on the cattle trail. The tales were lively and amusing, filling the room with warmth and laughter.

* * *

Aenghas and Daidre stayed where they had found shelter for the night. There was good forage for the horses. They built a fire, ate the vittles Ailene had prepared for them, and stayed relatively dry. The air was cold, however, robbing them of sleep. At first light they pressed on to town. They expected to arrive in Carter before noon. It had been an intense storm. The water was still standing in the low-lying terrain and puddled in the washes through which the road traversed. The wind began to gust and swirl again.

At last they arrived in Carter. The streets were still swamped and muddy. The wagon wheels left deep ruts in the miry clay, even unladed as it was. Aenghas drove the team to the livery to rest them while he and Daidre finished their business.

Smithy came out and greeted his brother with a robust laugh and vigorous hand shake. Daidre smiled at these two grown men acting as if they were twelve.

"Maiddie will be so glad to see ya," Smithy said to her. "We'll see to the horses. Now, why don't you go see your aunt. You haven't been to town for a while. There's probably much to catch up on."

She gracefully dismounted, gave him a hug, and skipped out of the livery to their house behind the stables. The yard was well tended, and in the cool autumn, flowers still grew along the walls of the two-story whitewashed cottage. Aunt Maiddie was behind the house, hanging clothes on the line. Daidre spoke and Maiddie immediately ran to greet her with a hug and a gentle kiss on her forehead.

"How is everyone?" she asked. "Is Ailene well? I haven't seen Graeme for a long time now. He must be getting so big. Is he, what, twelve now?" Each time Daidre tried to respond, Maiddie would ask another question. After an awkward pause, they both laughed at the absurd conversation.

"Come in for some tea, dear. Then we can visit more," Maiddie said. Toting the basket under one arm and the other wrapped around Daidre, she led the way to the house.

Aenghas and Smithy unhitched the team and led them along with Daidre's horse to stalls, as always, prepared with fresh straw. They filled the mangers with hay. The horses ate contentedly while the men sat with coffee and caught up on the news and gossip.

"You know those horses I bought were supposed to be delivered by now," Aenghas said. "I can't believe the men Daegan dealt with would do anything to deceive me, but I've had no word from them since late summer. They assured me that Thomas would bring them out as agreed. I honestly think something has gone wrong. I'm going to wire Mathias in Collyre to see if he has seen them."

Smithy offered a flask of "mist," which Aenghas accepted, pouring a jigger of it into the coffee. "The sheriff got a telegram from Mat a couple of days ago warning us of some men that might be headed this way. A bad lot they are, from what the telegram says, but nothin' 'bout horses. The train came in the other afternoon. There were no horses on it."

"Well, that doesn't sound good," said Aenghas. "Still, I should like to know what has become of the young fellow, and I am anxious to see the horses. The mare, I believe, will be a great addition to my, er, ranching ambitions." He chuckled. "I didn't think I'd get hooked on it so, but I have done well thus far."

"Davis is trying to get some of the men ready if trouble does come," Smithy said. "Can we count on you, Aenghas, if it comes to it?"

"Of course. You know that, Daenny, m' boy." Aenghas raised his cup in cheerful salute. "But first I'm going to see Charlie." He clapped a hand on Smithy's shoulder and hurried out the door.

"We'll be meetin' at the café at four o'clock!" Smithy called after him.

With a wave of acknowledgment, Aenghas strode to the train station and the telegraph office.

XIII

Thomas sat on the cot in the hay shed waiting for he knew not what. This was a precarious position to be in. He had never before doubted himself, but now, strangely, he searched for courage and strength. His side throbbed. He lay down trying to rest, but questions raced through his mind without answers. A wave of dread flooded his heart when, from the livery, he heard a familiar voice. He had tangled with that man and had been bested. It was now a few years ago, but it still haunted him. The other voice was foreign to him. His was a smooth, rhythmic, aristocratic sort, but laced with a sinister malice.

"Where is Tuck?" he whispered in the shadows.

Then he heard a deep bellowing voice. "What can I do fer you gents?"

"We'll need to stable our horses," the colonel said eloquently.

"It'll be two bits a day," said Whit.

"Fair enough. We'll be movin' on in a couple of days. By the way, have you seen this man?" He pulled a poster from his jacket pocket.

Whit studied it for a moment. He looked into the stranger's eyes with suspicion. "No, can't say that I have," he said. "What's he done?"

"He killed a deputy of mine sometime back. We've trailed him here, thus far."

"Oh. Well, where are the horses?" Whit asked nonchalantly.

"We'll be bringing them by later," the colonel said with a gentlemanly drawl. He tipped his hat and the men turned to go.

Remembering what Tuck had said, Whit called to them as they were leaving the livery. "You know, there was a fella came through a few days ago. I never saw him up close, but I haven't seen him around since. This is a small town, no place to hide."

The colonel stopped and turned to Whit. "You know, that's what the sheriff said." He turned abruptly and walked away.

Whit stood in the door of the livery and watched the men head down the street. When they had gone into the saloon, he turned and finished feeding the occupants in the livery.

Thomas had listened to the men but hadn't been able to completely decipher what was said. After a time, he heard heavy boots clomp to the door of the hay shed. He drew his gun as the latch was lifted.

"Mister," Whit said before entering, "I'm a friend of Tuck. He told Miss Mallory you were hiding out here." He opened the door and stepped inside. Recognizing Tom's face from the poster he said, "Those men are after you. They seem to have all the right papers, but somethin' just don't add up. What is it that you done, 'sides killin' a deputy?"

Thomas chose his words carefully. "The fella I killed was no deputy but an assassin from a ruthless brotherhood of hired killers. I was minding my own business, but it seems they didn't cotton to the Bible I had on the table. He drew first but with careless aim. I guess after I left, they convinced everyone there that I was a murderin' thief. I didn't stick around to defend myself, bein' greatly outnumbered." After a moment he asked, "Did they say who they were?"

"One says he's a colonel of some sort, a real smooth talker. The other claims to be a reverend," answered Whit. "He don't act like no reverend."

Thomas grimaced, recalling their first meeting. After considering the news, he said, "I'm not ready to face these men. My whereabouts must remain secret. James is in grave danger and doesn't realize what these barbarians are capable of."

"Who's James?" Whit asked, a bit confused.

"He's my brother. We've only found each other recently after many years of being apart. We went separate ways after a petty quarrel. Now, it seems fate has brought us together at long last." Thomas shifted his position to ease the pain. "This wound in my side is beginning to hurt again. Ma Parker said the doc should look after it. Can you get her to come by without being spotted?"

"Tuck left a note for Miss Mallory," Whit said, checking the wound. "It looks a bit like it needs some tendin'. I'll heat some water, at least, and help you clean it up. The doctor is tied up with those other fellas. We don't want to lead them here to you if we can help it. Maybe she can stop by later tonight." Whit stepped out to Tuck's room to fetch some water. After a time, he returned with a pan of steaming water and clean cloths to bathe the wound.

Thomas had had time to think about his new friends. "Who is Ma Parker?" he asked bluntly. "She has some strange ways about her. What do all those leaves and berries do?"

Whit chuckled sharing in Tom's sentiment. "She came here a few years ago or so. She lived in a cave up on the bluff. Some nights there'd be a fire so big we could see it from town. Strange goin's on fer shore. The scavengers would flock to the mesa and circle for hours like a big black cloud. The next minute they'd be gone. After a time, she'd just show up in the store, pick up a few things, and be gone just as quick. The widow at the boardin' house asked her to come stay and help out. When the widow packed up and headed back east, she gave the whole thing to Ma Parker. About a month ago, she started acting strange, sayin', "There's a nor'easter comin'. Better get ready.""

"So, what's Tuck's story?" Thomas asked. "He seems to have some gift of insight that don't make much sense."

"Don't rightly know," Whit said, scratching his head. "He came here with Ma Parker as I hear tell. Just gets along with her and helps out with the chores. They're an odd pair, fer certain," he chuckled.

"She got spooked sayin' somethin' about the colonel comin'," said Thomas. "Said she was goin' up to the mesa and hide out for a while until he left."

"You know, Tuck was actin' a mite strange when he left the note for Miss Mallory," Whit said. "I best be gettin' back to check on her. Clayton and Bart prob'ly need to get back to the LV Bar B." As he stepped to the door he said, "I'll see to it the doctor comes in later when it's safe." He slipped out the door quietly. After checking all the horses in the livery, Whit hurried to Dr. Murphy's house.

Thomas drifted off to sleep, but his dreams haunted him. He woke with a start when someone stirred outside the hay shed.

It was dark when Whit returned. He lit a lantern in Tuck's room and went around to the stalls and checked the horses. He stoked the fire in the stove. Then he stepped to the hay shed to check on Thomas.

"Miss Mallory is going to bring some food for ya," Whit said. "How's that wound doin'? Let me see, now. She gave me some salve to put on it. Here's a bit of whiskey to take the edge off. Just a bit now, it's pretty stout." Whit chuckled and handed the flask to Thomas.

When he'd finished dressing the wound, he took some of the hay and fed the horses. The bay nickered softly. He assured Thomas that he would return with Miss Mallory.

Thomas took a draft from the flask. It warmed his chest as it slid down his throat. He felt dazed. The walls of the shed swirled, distorted and wavering. Then all was dark. He awoke suddenly as the door creaked open. His vision still blurred, he strained to look at the figure stooping over him.

A handsome woman spoke gently to ease his distress. "The fever has clouded your senses," she whispered. "You'll be all right." She wiped his brow with a cool cloth.

"I'm cold," Thomas said, shivering. "I miss the warmth of Ma Parker's room, the fragrance of the purple flowers, and the sound of the flickering fire. The days seem endless." Lightning flashed, and the rumbling thunder reminded him of the night in the cave on the mesa.

"I've made arrangements for the other men to board in the hotel. Their associates hopefully will be leaving soon. Whit will bring you to the house when it is safe," she said. "Your wound will not take your life, but I fear your soul is wearied by despair. Come, take some soup and bread. It will warm your body and strengthen your spirit." She looked deep into his eyes. There was kindness and goodness in this man that was absent in the others she cared for. Wiping his brow again, she spoke. "We'll—I mean, *you'll* be okay soon," she said as she stood up to go.

Thomas reached for her arm. "I've sent my brother on a perilous course. I must be well enough to ride soon."

He was determined to leave after the colonel and the reverend were gone. It would be best to follow them to keep an eye on them. It was the only way to help James.

XIV

James relaxed, mesmerized, by the steady sway of the train rolling along the tracks in time with the rhythm of the wheels clacking over the seams. The horses stood with their heads bowed low. They blinked their eyes lazily. They too rested, lulled by the monotonous motion. The sunlight flickered through the slats of the stock car. In the warmth, James felt his tense muscles relax and his joints, stiff from the cold, move more easily. Yet the crisp breeze filled the stock car with fresh air.

After a time, he stretched, putting his hands under his head contemplating his next move. He wondered about the men Dudley had described, who were now staying in Collyre. He assumed they had a part to play in this game of hide-and-seek. Calculating that it would take an hour to reach the ravine, he checked the horses, loaded his pistols and rifle, and filled the cartridge belt. The mare nickered to him softly and nudged his chest with her muzzle. She licked her lips and pulled on the ties in her stall. She was eager to go. The door at the front of the car slowly opened. James turned quickly, drew his pistol, locking the hammer into firing position. He relaxed his stance when Dudley stepped in carrying a steaming cup.

"Another twenty minutes and we will be at the ravine," he said. "Here's some coffee for you before you go. The train will have to stop at the water tank a couple of miles past the trestle. You can get off then."

"Ma Parker said I was to find the trail that drops into the canyon. Do you know what she was talking about?" James asked.

"I don't know of anyone deliberately going into the ravine," Dudley replied. "Are you sure she meant *the* ravine?"

"She said it was a difficult path but one I must take. She also said she would guide me, whatever that means."

"Well, that is rightly strange," Dudley said, chuckling. "Still, I'd listen to every sound, if that's what she told you. If it were anyone else sayin' those things, I'd pay no mind, but since she told you, I'd believe it."

James thanked Dudley for the coffee and sat in deep thought until the train began to slow. He peeked through the slats as the train crossed over a deep gorge. The trusses of the trestle creaked and groaned as the heavy locomotive slowly but steadily eased over the gorge. The engine puffed and chugged along the track. Dudley stood still in silence until the hollow sound of the wheels quickened and resumed the rhythmic clack on solid ground.

"It won't be long now," he said at last. He turned and stepped out the door to go about his chores. After a time, the train began to slow again. As it approached the water tank, the engineer announced the stop with a long blare of the whistle. Dudley returned to the stock car and helped James get the horses ready to unload. When the train stopped, Dudley lowered the ramp from the stock car. Steam poured out from under the engine as it idled, while the scuttleman climbed the ladder to the water tank platform.

James unloaded the horses and led them to a trough beneath the water tank. The horses drank willingly. Some of the passengers stepped off the train to stretch. James offered a hand to Dudley. "Thanks," he said, stepping into the stirrup. As he swung into the saddle, he noticed two men standing beside the passenger car looking intently at him. Realizing they seemed to recognize him, he spurred the mare forward, cutting in front of the locomotive. He galloped across the plain and headed for a draw some distance away. He looked back only once. The men stood and watched him ride away. He dropped into the draw, then slowed his pace. He knew they wouldn't follow yet; there were no other horses on the train. But he was sure they would meet again.

It was late afternoon when the train pulled away from the water tank. James was well rested and rode at an easy pace back to the ravine. There was a trail leading into the canyon that he had to find, hopefully before dark. The blare of the whistle faded. The train chugged westward to Carter.

Continuing toward the ravine, James noticed a flock of scavengers circling overhead. There, in the draw just ahead of him, was the carcass of a deer. As he approached, a cougar sprang from behind it, hissing and yowling. The horses reared in fright and pulled on the leads. The mare tried to turn and escape as the big cat ran into the ravine, leaping from boulder to boulder, disappearing as if magically. He settled the horses. The scavengers squawked noisily and landed not far from the carcass.

At the rim of the ravine, James scouted the land for possible trails. There didn't seem to be any. He heard the roar of the river far below and saw the white spray and shimmering rainbows against the wet granite at the bottom. The horses snorted at the scent the cat had left behind. He eased the mare along the edge of the ravine, looking desperately for the trail Ma Parker had insisted he should find. After searching for some time, a cold gust of wind came up a draw. A dust devil rose from the rim, twisting across the plain and dissipating as quickly as it had begun.

There seemed to be a narrow path sloping gently into the ravine. Along its edges, scrub brush grew. There was just enough space for a horse to pass. There would be no way to turn back once he dropped into the canyon. "This has to be it," he mumbled. He let the mare pick her way through the rocks. She held her head low to the trail and carefully eased over and around the boulders.

"This isn't much of a trail," he mused, but he urged the mare forward. The others followed reluctantly. They pulled on the leads, jerking James off-balance. At that, the mare stopped and waited for him to right himself again.

The shadows in the ravine were beginning to lengthen, stealing the last spark of daylight as he continued down to the bottom. The roar of the water grew louder, and the air was crisp and damp. A mist rose from the water rushing over the great boulders in the midst of the river. Twilight seemed to overtake the shadows, and darkness consumed them. Still, the mare pressed on with her head low to the ground. At last they came to the river's edge. The canyon had opened up, and the river flowed deep and silent. Where granite boulders had been a moment before, the bank was now a bog of sand. The horses labored through the mire but came at last to a lush green meadow. He could still hear the distant roar of the Bullrim rushing to the valley floor, but all else was silent. He gently pulled on the reins. The mare stopped willingly. Her weary muscles quivered, but she bent her head to munch the green grass. The other horses ate hungrily. James sat and listened to the night wind. No sound rose above the babbling of the river. After resting the mare, he continued along the Bullrim.

Late into the night, he finally stopped in a stand of aspen and pines. He had grazed the horses enough, so he tethered them to the trees. He pulled the saddle from the mare. She rolled in the soft grass and shook the weariness from her back. He felt safe here in this quiet valley.

James slept until the mare nickered softly, as the morning crept back into the valley. The birds began to sing and chirp merrily, flitting among the branches of the currant bushes. He awoke refreshed and stepped to the edge of the woods. He led the horses out and grazed them under a shroud of dense fog. A spring trickled and tumbled over moss-covered stones. It seemed like heaven would look like this. James was at peace and allowed nothing to intrude upon the serenity. The sun rose over the rim of the canyon, chasing the fog from the meadows. Slowly it crept out of the canyon and up the draws, until it melted away to reveal the cerulean sky.

The horses munched quietly on the grass, swatting at the occasional flies and blowing the dust from their nostrils. James inspected their legs for any cuts from the rocks on the canyon trail. The mare had a trickle of blood from her right hind fetlock. It didn't amount to much, but he bathed it in the stream anyway. After a time, he returned to where he had camped. He settled in for a day of quiet thought. The horses needed the rest and so did he.

Leaving the horses in the shelter of the wooded draw, he took his rifle and headed upstream to find its source. The water ran icy cold. It babbled over the small granite stones. The way became rockier and steep. Above the valley floor, he perched upon a ledge where the waterfall splashed over the crag below. In the distance to the west, he could see rows of smoke rising and mingling with the dusty air. He surmised that the town lay about twenty miles away, more or less. The guessing game he and Thomas had played in their childhood now proved relevant.

The valley veered to the north, where taller peaks stood as sentries with their white caps glistening like diamonds in the sun. The tree line was shimmering with gold and silver among the lush pine forest. The air was fresh and fragrant as he drew a deep breath. He closed his eyes. "Can you smell them?" Recalling Ma Parker's description of this valley. How could there be any better place on earth, he wondered. The sun passed noon and began to swing westward. After a time, he made his way back to the shelter of the thicket and the horses. Building a small fire, he heated some coffee and ate some of the cakes and jerky he had stowed in his saddlebags. The songbirds were silent, yet an occasional drone from the night birds beckoned the shadows to lengthen. A prairie wolf yapped and in the silence waited for an answer from a distant knoll. The chirping of the crickets was the last sound James heard in the night. Blowing dust from their nostrils, the horses too drowsed in the serene shelter of the thicket.

Just before dawn, the mare nickered and began to fidget and stomp. James awoke to the horse's discontent. Looking up at the morning sky he gazed, for a while, at the stars still twinkling brightly in the crisp autumn air. The breeze was from the north. He thought about his brother and pondered the events that had taken him on this adventure. He led the horses into the meadow to graze them for a short time before continuing westward. The wind began to gust and blow, whistling through the pines and rattling the leaves of the aspens, tugging at them until they fluttered from the grasp of the limbs. Twirling and spinning by the command of an invisible partner, they tossed and turned before settling gently on the ground. A pair of scavengers flew overhead, squawking loudly, then disappeared beyond a bend in the river. James stepped into the stirrup, looked quickly behind him, and urged the mare westward along the Bullrim.

As he rode, he began to develop a plan. The men he'd seen as he rode from the train had to be dealt with. He wished Thomas was with him. Still, he had at least twenty miles, a day's ride or more, before he had to face the enemy. The scavengers circled around again, swooping toward the horses with their emphatic squawks, then flying erratically away. Swirling without a course the wind blew James's hat from his head. He stopped the mare and began to dismount. He was suddenly struck on the side of his head. All went dark as he hit the ground. Thunder rumbled in his memory. The mare ran off a short distance and stopped. The young horses ran wildly, bucking with fright. James knew nothing more.

XV

Dudley returned to his chores when James had gone. He sensed that he was a good man with a snake biting at his heels. He turned and saw the men staring at James as he rode away. He memorized their faces, just in case. Pretending to pay them no mind, he brushed past them. One of them pushed him down.

"You're gettin' too nosey, boy," he rasped.

Dudley got up and brushed the dirt from his sleeve. He looked hard at the man but said nothing. He scurried back to the stock car.

The engineer and scuttleman finished filling the boiler with water as the engine puffed in a rhythm all its own. Steam escaped in time with a hiss from beneath the great "iron horse". The men stood by the passenger car, watching James disappear over the distant knoll. They pulled their pistols and checked the cylinders and firing mechanisms. One, answering only to Dex, twirled the ivory-grip pistol and slid it gently into the holster. The men looked at each other and, without a word, boarded the train.

As the train lurched forward they strained their eyes in the direction the rider had gone, intently waiting for one last glimpse of him and the three horses that had slipped away. They had only to be patient, assuming they would meet up with him at an appointed time. Facing each other in their seats, Dex pulled a deck of cards from his shirt pocket while the other, Vic, as he was named, rolled a cigarette out of a bag of "fixin's" from his coat. They had ridden together since childhood and thought alike in these schemes for which they were hired. Their nods and gestures went unnoticed by the other passengers, but between them, their evil intentions were clear. There was time still, so they relaxed and drew no attention to themselves. It would be well into the night when they reached Carter. They'd work out the details of the ambush at the hotel.

One of the passengers, a dapper fellow with thick glasses, overheard their subtle conversation and suggested that perhaps he could arrange for the horses they needed. He would speak to someone who may be willing to provide them. He would have this particular person meet them at the saloon.

The train moved along at a rhythmic pace. The engineer had a schedule to keep and hoped to pull into the Carter station at 8:00 p.m. Being a bit behind schedule, he urged the scuttleman to stoke the fire for the boiler.

At 8:15 p.m. the train eased up to the depot. After the passengers stepped down, the engineer pulled the train forward to the switchyard. There the train was eased onto the wye track where it was filled with water and wood for the return trip east. The crew slept in the bunkhouse, and the local café supplied a good meal. There was a boiler that heated water for them to freshen up with. The crew would spend the next day tidying the passenger coach and loading the baggage car with mail and goods to return east.

Dex and Vic retrieved their saddles from the baggage car. Vic headed for the telegraph office to send a wire to Collyre. When he had completed his task, he went to the hotel. Dex went to the saloon. There he hoped to meet with the man who'd furnish them with horses.

Dex stepped onto the boardwalk. He clomped noisily through the swinging doors of the saloon. The smoke-filled room had a robust atmosphere. It was well lit, and the ladies made sure the revelers were cared for in every way. One such gal strolled up to Dex with a jigger in hand and offered it to him, fixated on his dark eyes. She was a sassy beauty wearing a tight red dancing dress. A black plume and rhinestones graced her auburn hair. He took the drink and slid his arm around her waist as she escorted him to a table near the back of the room. As he passed the bar, he gave a nod to one of the patrons who raised his glass in salute. Not giving anything away, Dex became engulfed in the merriment. At closing time, he bid his fair lady farewell and staggered into the street. Looking both directions, he acquainted himself with the main street of town. He located the hotel and began to walk toward it. He slipped into the alley, however, when no one seemed to take notice.

Being more sober than what he pretended, he circled back to the rear of the saloon to meet up with the fellow he had toasted earlier. With the stranger was a fellow who had the horses that were requested. There was a gully in a stand of trees just a short distance west of town, out of sight of the road. They would be in a make-shift corral. The deal and payment were agreed upon and the men parted, strangers once more. Dex went to the hotel and rented a room. There, he and Vic would bide their time. The man they pursued still had a long way to travel in an open valley. They would have the advantage for an ambush.

Before daylight, Dex and Vic slipped out of town to pick up the horses and head back to kill the man they had watched ride from the water tank the day before. They followed the railroad tracks but stayed out of sight. They rode all day and long into the night before camping on the open plain. Weary from the ride, they rode out from camp later the next morning. The sun shone high over head when they reached the water tank and picked up the trail of their contract. The tracks were beginning to fade from the afternoon breezes blowing across the sandy soil. A pair of scavengers flew overhead and folded their wings to dip down into the valley below the edge of the bluff. They shifted their heads from side to side squawking noisily.

A few scrub juniper trees grew along the edge of the bluff. There the men stopped and surveyed the valley. They dropped to the ground at almost the exact instant. There below was the man they had been hired to kill. They tied the horses to a tree away from the edge and belly crawled until they reached a runoff draw. Silently they crept through the gouges dug deep into the side of the bluff. It would be a long shot. They had to try to scramble closer. Halfway down the bluff was a ledge that would conceal them and grant them an advantage. The element of surprise was in their favor. They both benched up on the sandy mounds and waited for a good shot. The wind gusted around them.

In the distance, the scavengers swooped down on the rider below. Just as the rifle echoed its report, the man fell from his horse. The gray mare ran a short distance and stopped, looking back at the man who lay face down. The other horses bolted away, running wildly along the river. The two men climbed back up the hill. They were puffing and gasping for air when they reached the top. The descent had been easier.

They reached the horses just as a storm began to roll through the valley. The lightning crackled and skipped through the clouds, and the thunder rumbled in the distance as the storm drew near. The riders moved quickly toward town once again. Looking back one last time, the men saw the mare standing over the body of the man they had killed. Soon the rain and wind would wash away their tracks. They took cover in a small stand of junipers and set out when the sun began to rise. They were cold and irritable.

It was late and pitch-dark when they rode into the gully where the horses had been corralled three days before. They dismounted and were unsaddling the horses when a voice from the shadows hollered over the downpour.

"Yer late!" he shouted. "I've been waitin' here near three hours. The Mrs. is gonna have my hide fer shore." He led the horses away and left Dex and Vic standing in ankle-deep mud. As they pulled their slickers across their chests, Dex called after him, "We may be needin' 'em again soon!" The man waved a hand as he disappeared into the dark. Vic and Dex shouldered the saddles and made their way back to the hotel. The rain continued throughout the night, with an occasional clap of thunder and flashes of lightning.

They would lay low a few days and take the stage back to Collyre.

XVI

To Thomas, the days seemed a drudgery. The air remained damp and cool. There was an occasional drizzling rain. Whit had finally helped him to the doctor's place. The colonel and the reverend had gone at last. Thomas gained in strength once again, now that he was in a place of solace and warmth. The town returned to the normal routine of everyday life. Thomas found it easy to talk with Mallory and bared much of his life to her. He told her about the men who'd followed him to Collyre and who were now bent on killing James. She listened intently, understanding his anguish as she shared the stories of her own struggles because of conflicts that seemed so long ago.

Thomas knew all too well that there was trouble brewing. His thoughts often fell to his brother. His dreams were haunted by murky visions of scattering horses, the wild look of terror in their eyes. He awoke to the echo of a distant rifle shot in the depths of his mind. The thunder boomed as he sat up in bed, trembling. He heard footsteps scurry down the hall. Whit opened the door and Mallory entered, pulling her robe around her.

"What is it, Mr. Atwell?" she asked as she hurried to his side.

Thomas sat on the edge of the bed, searching for his boots and hat.

"I have to go," he stated firmly. "James is in trouble." He winced as he got to his feet, still a bit unsteady. Whit caught his arm and helped him to stand.

"Can't it wait till morning?" Mallory whispered as she stroked his forehead with gentle fingers. Whit helped him back into bed. Mallory offered a quaff of a bitter drink that seemed to melt the anxiety he felt. She sang softly in a faraway voice. Thomas struggled to stay awake but succumbed to the sedative. In a dream, he walked down a dimly lit stairway into a damp cavern. He heard the echoes of dripping water and the jingle bobs of his spurs. He breathed in deeply the fragrance of lavender that he remembered from Ma Parker's house. For a time, he lay quiet and slept. The flicker of the distant candle snuffed out leaving his conscience suspended in a void of empty recess.

The sun rose brightly against the pale blue sky. A rooster crowed just outside the window. Thomas awakened and was captivated by Mallory's deep gray eyes. They seemed to be smiling at him, and he returned the gesture. The aroma of coffee replaced, at once, the scent of lavender that had filled the room last night. His strength had indeed returned to him. He was glad he had heeded the doctor's advice.

Thomas dressed and packed a few things into the saddlebags. He smelled bacon sizzling on the stove. He stepped into the kitchen. It was as though he belonged there. Mallory handed him a plate and dished up a fine breakfast. Whit sat in the corner grinning, yet never saying what was on his mind. He watched this friendship develop right before his eyes. "Finally," he thought to himself. "Here might be the man she has waited for." He rose from the table and served himself.

"Oh, I'm sorry, Whit. I must have forgotten my manners," Mallory confessed.

Whit chuckled. "It's okay, Miss Mallory. You jest 'tend to your guest." He clapped a hand on Thomas's shoulder and sat down to eat his breakfast.

The conversation continued to late morning. At long last, Thomas pulled his watch from his pocket. "Eleven o'clock," he said out loud. "I best be gettin' on."

Mallory smiled, but her eyes reflected the sadness that filled her heart. "Perhaps, you could return to me...er...I mean to Collyre for a visit...you know, sometime," she stammered. "Well, Whit, please help Mr. Atwell with whatever he needs." Embarrassed at this outburst, she hurried down the hall beyond the parlor and up the stairs.

Whit exchanged a quick glance with Thomas and nodded toward the door. "Her room is second on the right."

Thomas slowly opened the door as he knocked gently. Mallory wiped a tear from her cheek and sniffled as he entered. She turned to look into his eyes. Before she could look away, he wrapped his arms around her and held her close to his chest. Her sobs melted into him as she pressed ever deeper into his arms. He felt as if he were taking all of her burden upon him and hoped she would replace it with joy.

After a time, he released her and held her fingers to his lips. "I will return to you, Mallory," he whispered. "Watch the western sky. There will be storms, and then a warm wind will blow through your beautiful hair. My fingers will brush away your tears. As true as this moment, I will return. Wait for me." He pressed his lips to her forehead and gently kissed her. With one last embrace, he left her there, yearning for yet another.

Whit had gone to the livery to fetch the bay Thomas was going to ride. Dudley was going about his usual chores, working around the livery while the train continued east.

"Where's Tuck? " he asked Whit. "His bunk hasn't been slept in."

"He and Ma are still up on the bluff, I believe. Don't know what got 'em all ruffled up, but somethin' about that colonel fella makes my hair hackle up too."

"There were some bad men on that train. They seemed a mite interested in that Thomas fella. You know, him that had the gray mare?" Dudley picked at the stalls. "Whose horse is that?" he asked as Whit saddled up the bay.

"A man that got hurt, and Miss Mallory patched 'im up. He's headin' south to beat the cold, I s'pect." Whit said no more to dispel Dudley's intuitive observations.

Whit led the bay to the doctor's house and waited outside. Thomas strapped on his guns, stepped off the porch and into the street. Looking west far beyond the last house, He sheathed his rifle into the scabbard, stepped into the stirrup and swung into the saddle. Mallory stood on the porch, holding tightly to the shawl that wrapped around her shoulders. He tipped his hat and offered a hand to Whit, a gesture of farewell.

"It would be best to head south to the Cedars," said Whit. "It's about twenty miles. There's no safe crossing of the Bullrim any farther north, since you're not going by train. You will have to swim the river, for it is deep and wide. It's calm water this time of year, though. It's a mite farther to Carter, but maybe they won't expect it. That colonel fella and the reverend went on the stage to Northford. Most likely they'll be going on to Carter. Dudley told me there were some men on the train that took an interest in your brother, so be careful. Use the name Nathan Navarr. I'll wire Smithy to put you up in the livery."

Thomas turned the bay south and spurred him into a lope. As he rode away, Whit called to him, "Rest your horse before you cross the river! The current is still strong, and the stud will labor to get to the other side."

It had rained the night before—the kind of rain that fills every runoff draw and creek bed. Deep pools of mud lingered as Thomas rode away. The alley by the jail concealed his departure. Beyond the railroad tracks, the gully offered cover from any who would be watching from the hotel. What Thomas didn't take into consideration was the man in the jail cell who watched silently as he crossed the tracks.

Thurman hissed, clenching his fists around the bars of the window. Vicious ranting spewed from his mouth, cursing the sheriff. Mathias ignored the tirade. He simply shut the door that separated the cells from the office.

The bay cantered contentedly along the winding wash. The muddy soil under his feet gave way generously. Thomas liked this horse with his easy gait and willing confidence. In his mind, he reflected on his childhood, and recognized this same trait in all the horses his father had raised. There were, however, none that measured up to the gray mare, with regard to her uncanny wariness. Knowing James was well mounted, he hoped all would go well with their plan. The wash veered westward toward the mesa. Thomas decided to follow it a bit longer before heading around the southern edge of it. As he neared the mesa, the dark clouds boiled and black scavengers circled high over head noisily straining against the downdrafts of the stiff wind. A piercing chill, swirled from the north, tugging at his coat. A dust devil whistled past him and up a draw. The delirious scavengers, frantically flew away without course or purpose. Thomas was left in a stillness that made his very soul shiver with dread. Then the sun shone brightly again, bringing with it a warmer breeze.

"This is a strange country," he heard himself say. The bay nickered softly, as if in agreement.

When he left the wash, heading farther south, the greasewood grew thick and gnarled. The bay picked his way through it, but Thomas still felt the tug of the thorns on his chaps. Some brambles grew so tall that his coat was tangled in the briers. The spines were sharp and occasionally pierced the canvas coat, poking his arm. After a time, the greasewood grew sparsely. The scrub brush and prickly pear cactus spread out across the sand. Dunes began to rise and fall with the shifting wind. The sand whirled around the horse's feet, rippling across the dunes to their crests, lingering in a cloud of dust, and sifting silently to the ground, forming a cornice in linear fashion. The landscape was ever changing, it seemed. He listened to what sounded like the eerie music of a violin reverberating above the hissing sand. Was it his imagination?

Thomas thought of the mazes of a circus, where doors were opened and closed, revealing different paths to the prize hidden in the very center of it. He had no idea what lay before him. He knew only that his route would take him to Carter—eventually. He somehow felt safe in this desert, yet was hoping to find enough water to make it that far. Whit had assured him that there was a spring beyond the spire of an ancient mountain split apart in a great explosion.

"It stands like an ominous watchman just at the far edge of the dunes," Whit had said. "There is a stand of trees at the bottom of a granite ridge where there is good forage for your horse and shelter from the impending storm. You will be able to rest there. It is a two-day ride."

The sun shone brightly and reflected off the desert sand. Thomas rested the bay and gave him water from the canteen. He had brought three upon Whit's advice. He drank only a bit, wetting his lips. He left the greater amount for his horse. He rode on into the night. After the crescent moon rose, he stopped to sleep for a few hours. The chill of the night opposed the heat of the day. He shivered with the thought that he would have no fire to warm him against the cold. This place seemed familiar to him, somehow. He dismounted taking the bedroll from behind the saddle and huddled in the wool blanket Whit had given him. Thomas slept very little.

Overcome by a heavy weight he couldn't explain, he slipped from consciousness, beneath a shadow of dread. It was as if he had been to this place before, but without memory. He imagined the spire that Whit had spoken of. He saw his brother and the men that he was sure pursued him. Yet, in his dream, he saw all of it dissolve into fine dust, blown away by the cold desert night wind. The vision took him back to the night he lay injured in the cave on the mesa. It seemed like the story of his life was rewritten, similar to but not the same as how he remembered it.

Just before dawn, the bay nickered softly. Thomas awoke with a start at the realization that he had nodded off. The bay stood a ways off. Thomas found it difficult to get to his feet. He ached all over. His muscles were stiff from the cold, and his fingers were numb and tingling. His head hurt, swimming with a drunken stupor of exhaustion. The bay shivered against the cold breeze. Thomas reached for the reins and decided to walk a bit to regain his balance and ward off the cold. He pulled some oat cakes and the bottle of whiskey from his saddlebags. The stud ate the cakes while Thomas sipped from the flask. After eating the jerky and cornbread Mallory had fixed, he felt strength return to him once again.

With the rising of the sun, the chill seemed to melt from his bones. He began to move freely, and feeling returned to his fingers and toes. Mounting for another long day in the saddle, Thomas pondered the dream that had haunted him in the night.

"Why does this place seem so familiar?" he said aloud. A sudden gust of wind from behind him sent sand hissing across the crest of the dune up ahead. It rose into a dust devil, twisting and shifting gracefully, unfolding and sifting aimlessly to the ground.

As he rode on, he began to look for landmarks that were vivid in his memory. Perhaps he would find the spring Whit had told him about before those men discovered his scheme.

For a time, the dunes rose and fell with the rhythm of the desert wind. A great mesa of barren stone appeared in the distance. What he thought was a mirage of vague shadows now rose high above the sand and scrub vegetation. There before him, the spire reached out of the sand just as Whit had described. The core of it was a rusted red, and the base was strewn with the boulders and rocks of an ancient lava flow.

The earth began to transform from sand to soft, dusty clay. The edge of the horizon was blurred and quivering from the heat of the day as the sun inched to the west, stretching the shadows along the northern side of the mesa. Aspen groves and chokecherry bushes grew up along the foot of it, where shards and boulders of granite lay scattered about. The air was cool in the shadow cast by the massive wall of granite. The breeze whistled through the aspens that grew among the junipers, their leaves flitting and swishing against the ever-changing breeze in rhythm with his horse's windblown mane.

As he rode along, the ground became damp. He followed a narrow game trail up a wash. Dancing across glistening smooth stones, a trickle of water babbled and sparkled in the fading sunlight. The grass was still green and fragrant, despite the autumn chill. The trail wound through the aspen grove and rose steadily until it abruptly vanished at the foot of the granite wall. Seeping from the base of it was the source of the spring. The pool of water was ice cold and clear. The bay drank greedily. His ears swayed lazily with each swallow. Thomas joined him. The water burned in his throat as he drank. Addicted to the taste of pure water, he drank until his belly ached. The bay lifted his head and savored the last swallow before licking his lips. He swished his tail lazily against the gnats and set about eating the sweet grass that grew around the pool.

Thomas, wary of the danger behind him, tied the bay and went back down the trail to erase the tracks that would lead his adversaries to him. The bay nickered softly upon his return. Thomas led his horse away from the pool to find shelter, a place where he could watch for any sign of pursuit. There arose a stinging wind out of the east. The fallen leaves fluttered across the trail he followed. Behind him, an aspen shuddered, creaked, and snapped, crashing to the ground. At once, all was calm. Thomas could only think of the strange woman in Collyre. "Ma Parker," he whispered.

XVII

Graeme rose early in the morning. Fog lay heavy on the ranch. The yard was soggy from yesterday's storm. He fed the horses and chickens before saddling to go to the east pasture to check the horses. He hoped they had found shelter along the bluff and away from the river. Their favorite mare, "Maira," as they called her, was smart and always took care of herself. She hated inclement weather and would get out of the storm. The others always followed her lead.

Graeme went back into the house. Daegan was at the table sipping on a hot cup of coffee. A plate of cake and a second cup of coffee were laid on the table. The brothers made their plans while savoring the snack.

"I'll come with you, little brother," he said. "Will you saddle up BB for me? He needs a bit of a stretch."

"Sure," Graeme answered. He finished the cake and coffee and headed out to the barn. Daegan took a cup of coffee to his mother, telling her their plans.

"We're goin' to the east pasture to check the horses. I'm sure they made their way to the bluff. We should be back by noon or so. The boys and me—"

"The boys and I," tilting her head, she corrected the grammatical error.

"Yes, ma'am. We're gonna sort the cows when we get back."

The two brothers rode off together. The fog began to slowly dissipate as the sun rose higher in the sky. Soon, a bright azure blue spread overhead. The crisp air smelled of wet grass and damp soil. The fragrance of cedar filled their senses as they turned their horses north to the bluff. The horses jogged along on a loose rein. An hour had passed when they reached a gate into the east pasture. Daegan dismounted and opened it and led his horse through. Graeme followed. He took a field glass from his saddlebags and scanned the distant meadow. There was no sign of the horses. The river below sparkled in the bright sunlight. As in the yard at home, it had flooded its banks. A few ducks circled over the river and landed in the still waters that covered the meadow grass along the bank of the Bullrim. They rode on, talking about the weather and sorting cattle and plans for the future. The bluff became rockier and more rugged. They followed a game trail along the bottom and soon came to the washed-out caves where Graeme had expected to find the horses. Still, there was no sign of them.

The sun rose higher in the sky, and quickly the morning turned to noon. They stopped to rest the horses. They dismounted and grazed them while they scanned the pasture for the missing horses. Graeme climbed the bluff to get a better look at the Bullrim valley.

From this vantage point Graeme could see to the very edge of the pasture. "There they are," he called to Daegan. "They are just where the Bullrim comes out of the gorge."

Just as he spoke, a pair of ravens swooped past him, squawking furiously. They flitted and dove into the valley and disappeared in the trees just beyond the horses. The startled horses scattered when, at that moment, Graeme caught sight of an unfamiliar horse. He quickly descended from the ledge and reported what he had seen. They mounted and rode into the valley heading in the direction of a gray horse. The other horses bolted past them as they approached. She stood motionless but pinned her ears as they dismounted and stepped toward the man over whom she stood. Daegan spoke softly to her, and she relaxed, stepping backward. She swished her tail and snorted, bending her head low to the ground, yielding to his persuasion. He checked her brand and then recognized her as the mare promised to be delivered with two others.

Graeme carefully turned the man to his back. James groaned and in some far-off place tried to respond. In his delusional state of mind, he swatted at the air, gripped a fistful of it, and fell limp again.

Daegan looked at his brother. "This is the man who was to deliver the horses last week. Father doesn't know his fate. We must get him back to the ranch and get word to him. Ride back to the ranch and get the buck." He hesitated. "Nah, Father took it."

"We could try to get him to the caves," said Graeme. "There is shelter there. You could ride to get Mother to come help. I'll stay with him until you get back with the wagon and Father. The horses don't seem to want to go anywhere. Maira will look after the new ones. Only that gray mare is bent on being with this fella."

They roused the stranger helping him to his feet and onto the gray. They rode with one on either side to steady him in the saddle. After a time, James woke enough to hold on to the saddle horn. The men decided to try to get to the ranch instead. They stopped several times to allow James to rest.

It was nearly dark when they, at last, rode into the yard. Ailene was sitting on the porch waiting for the boys to return. She rushed to the gate as they rode up still bracing the man on the gray mare. Daegan dismounted and helped him down. Stumbling forward, James fell into Ailene's arms. His limp weight knocked her to the ground. He groaned as he fell in a heap at her feet.

"Sorry, Mum," Daegan apologized.

Ailene got up and helped Daegan carry the man into the house. Graeme took the horses to the barn and settled them in. The mare ate and drank what he set before her, then lay down to rest her weary limbs. When Graeme was finished, he went to the room where Daegan and Ailene had taken the man.

James shivered with a fever. His dreams were haunted by places that he thought he had seen before. Ailene bathed the wound on his brow, cleaning the blood that had crusted on his eye and cheek. He fidgeted and mumbled incoherently. She managed to get him to sip whiskey to warm his body and numb his thoughts. Soon he lay quiet. His dreams began to fade away as sleep overtook him. The fog of the liquor clouded his memory all the more. He lay in shadows where images of faces emerged out of the mist. Some he knew while others he had seen yet not known. Even those faded from sight, leaving questions in his mind. He struggled to remember his own name. He would find himself wandering in a dark chasm. An incandescent glow came through a slit far above him. The pale blue light would pulsate in time with the beating of his heart. He felt a cool breeze waft across his face, then darkness enveloped his constricted world. The eerie dream replayed in fragmented sequence. On one particular occasion, however, he heard sweet music. The slit of light began to grow and come ever nearer. He heard voices that became more distinct. It was, he guessed, two women whispering. The sound would fluctuate as the shadows had earlier. At long last, the slit of light flooded his conscious thoughts. He felt his eyes flutter and squint against the brilliance. They opened suddenly, as if by their own decision. James blinked and breathed deeply, filling his lungs with a fresh start.

Surveying his surroundings, he squinted against the blinding light streaming through the window, illuminating the room in contrast to his dark dreams. An indistinct red halo encircled the blurred objects scattered about. A young woman came to his side to calm him. He couldn't focus on her face. It felt as if his eyes heeded no command but wandered aimlessly.

"You are safe," she whispered. "The horses are safe as well."

"What do you mean?" he managed to ask. "Who are you?"

"Just rest, now. It may come back to you soon."

She stepped back and closed the shade a bit to help him adjust to the light. Ailene came in at Daidre's bidding. Aenghas, who had been playing the bagpipes, stepped in behind her.

"Thomas, m'boy, it's good to see you. I was getting a bit worried and a bit skeptical, if I may say so," he said. "You rest up now. The horses are as fine as I expected." He turned and went back into the parlor again, blowing a hearty measure of notes on the bagpipe.

"But I am..." James was too tired to speak.

Daidre stirred a drink and helped James bring it to his lips. His head was swirling, and his eyes grew heavy. He again tried to mumble something but couldn't remember what he wanted to say. A slight smile crossed his lips. He relaxed in the warmth of the soft bed and fragrant morning air. He closed his eyes but listened to the women chatter beyond the bed. He heard the click of the latch, and the voices fade beyond hearing.

He awoke abruptly and sat up in bed. His head pounding, he lay back, grimacing in pain. Footsteps drew near to the door. A gentle tap on the door announced the return of the young woman. She carried with her a tray of soup and bread. She brightened the lantern that had been burning dimly for a while. He propped himself against the wall and ate the soup she had carefully set before him. His head began to clear. Waves of memory raced across his mind in images veiled and incomplete. How he had fallen from his horse remained a mystery to him, however. It annoyed him. Time had passed and night approached with no recollection of the day.

XVIII

The stage pulled into Northford at about five o'clock and was scheduled to stay overnight to rest the horses and passengers. It wasn't much more than a station, a place where the routes divided for travelers who were venturing farther north. That road was desolate and perilous. Eber Donn *"Dark Road"* was what the clans had named it. The southern fork, to Carter, was the only way around the gorge carved out by the Bullrim.

Mrs. Mueller cooked a fine meal for the passengers and driver. The horses were unhitched and corralled for the night. The house was warm and comfortable, with the musky scent of sage and baking bread filling the room. Mrs. Mueller showed the gentlemen to their rooms. They settled in and then joined the others in the parlor for conversation and libations. In the corner was a round table with a fresh deck of cards, inviting guests to play a friendly game of poker before turning in. No money was at stake. Each man was given the same amount of chips with which to play. The game would end at ten o'clock, no matter what. That was the rule.

Breakfast was at 7:00 a.m. sharp, and the stage would leave precisely at 8:00 a.m. Even so, it wouldn't get to Carter until five in the afternoon if all went well.

"All aboard!" shouted the driver. He and the guard loaded the bags and strapped the baggage compartment tightly. The mail and money pouch were secured in a strong box under the driver's seat. The guard checked his rifle and shotgun and then climbed to the top of the stage. Mrs. Mueller secured the doors and bid everyone farewell.

As the stage headed west, the thunderous roar of the torrent river grew ever more menacing. The road began to wind among massive boulders. The driver slowed the horses and eased the coach through the labyrinth of broken granite. Great shards of blackened stone were strewn about as a result of an explosion in time long beyond reckoning. There rose a mist from the deep canyon to the south of the road. The air was damp and heavy as the coach passed just north of the very beginnings of the great waterfall that was the Bullrim. The place was called Clach an Udalain, the *"Rolling Stone."* The passengers marveled at the beauty and power of the great river. The earth trembled beneath the stage wheels rumbling along the hardened track of the road.

Beyond the field of granite boulders, the driver urged the team into an easy lope, continuing at a rapid pace. A fleeting rainbow glistened in the mist and the roar of the falls became a far-off drone. The landscape was filled with prairie grass and occasional fragrant cedar trees. The driver slowed the horses as they approached another station along the route where the team of horses was changed before heading on into Carter. The passengers stretched as the caretaker and driver harnessed the new team. The colonel and the reverend took advantage of the opportunity to discuss the details of a sketchy plan to find and kill the Parson.

"Maybe we won't even have to do anything," the reverend said.

"Once we get to Carter, we'll check with Vic and Dex," the colonel replied. "We don't know for sure if this Parson fella has even gotten there yet. All the telegram said was that the objective was close at hand."

The stage was ready to continue on to Carter. The colonel checked his watch. "Two more hours," he grumbled aloud. He opened the cylinder of his pistol and rechecked the load. When he was satisfied, he holstered it and climbed aboard.

"Get up!" shouted the driver as he slapped the horses with the lines. There would be no more stops until Carter.

XIX

James slept well through the night and felt his strength return. It had been three days since the accident. The headache was now dull, something he could tolerate. He got to his feet and washed his face in the basin left on the dressing table. The water was cold and felt good on his throbbing head. He pulled on his boots and stepped out into the parlor. There seemed to be no one about as he made his way to the kitchen. The coffee pot was hot on the stove. There were cups sitting on a butcher block that invited him to help himself. He poured the coffee as Daidre entered from the porch.

"I'll be glad to join you," she said, the screen door snapping shut behind her. Her accent was a bit unusual but had a poetic rhythm to it that he liked.

"So where are you from? Originally, I mean," he asked as he sipped the coffee.

"Well, I was born here. So I guess that means I'm from here," Daidre mused.

They both laughed, but she continued, "My family is from across the sea to the east. Papa came here long ago and homesteaded before the others settled in Carter. He then sent for Mama. It took nearly a year for her to make it to her new home.

Aenghas and Daegan came in from morning chores. Daidre met them at the door with coffee.

Ailene followed them with her apron filled with eggs. "Well," she said to their guest. "Looks like you've a mite more color on your lips than you had yesterday. Are you hungry?"

Yes, ma'am," he said.

"So, Thomas, what kind of trouble are ya bringin' our way?" Aenghas was curious.

James was baffled. "That's not my name," he said. "I'm...I'm..." He pondered for a moment. "I can't remember my name."

Daegan stepped closer to him. "Aren't you the fella we bought the horses from last spring? Aren't you Thomas Atwell?"

James struggled within himself to remember who he was. "I know that name, but for some reason, I don't think that I am Thomas."

"Well, maybe it'll come to you someday," Ailene said. "You are welcome here, sir, however you want to be called. Since we don't know your name, perhaps you can pretend to be Thomas, at least for now."

"Can you tell us about your family?" asked Daidre. "Where do you come from?"

James began to tell them about his life. It amazed him that he could recall so many things that took place when he was a small child. He even remembered his grandfather and grandmother by name. He told them of his grief at the passing of his parents. He related his admiration for his uncles. He even expounded with great detail the disagreements he and his brother had up to the time that they separated, vowing to keep out of each other's way. Still, he could not recall his own name.

James became weary and excused himself, retiring to the bedroom. When he awoke, it was nearing dusk. Daidre had lit the lantern and set a tray of cake and milk on the nightstand. He sat on the edge of the bed and enjoyed the snack. He pulled on his boots and stepped out the door. The parlor was well lit and the glow of the fireplace warmed the room. Everyone was gathered around the table eating a dinner of chicken and mashed potatoes. Everywhere he ventured there was chicken and potatoes of some variation. He chuckled to himself at the thought. Ailene gestured to the chair across from Daidre. He sat down and ate heartily. There was laughter and jovial conversation here. After dinner, the men retreated to the parlor while the ladies cleaned up. Aenghas offered a draft of brandy to James and asked him about the horses. The gray mare in particular had drawn his interest.

"You know, the gray mare was very protective of you in the Bullrim valley where we found you," Daegan said. "It took a bit of convincing her that we were trying to help you. Are you sure you can part with her?"

"Ma Parker told me to keep the North Star in my right hand," James remembered. "She must have been talking about the mare. She is a very strange woman."

"Who's Ma Parker?" Graeme asked.

"Don't rightly know. She has an odd way about her. She knows things, suggests things, and communicates in a way that's just plum spooky, if ya catch my drift. She's the one who told me to drop down into the ravine, saying she'd let me know where. There were a lot of black scavengers everywhere I went, and those crazy whirligigs would just pop up out of nowhere. In fact, there were those birds swirlin' overhead when I came off the mare."

As he took a sip of brandy, pictures began to form in his mind.

"I remember there was a gust of wind that blew my hat off. I was just stepping down to pick it up. That's the last I remember, except the thunder. It seemed to echo long in my memory."

He had accomplished his mission, whatever it had been, he thought. He had delivered the horses to Aenghas Dougan. He wrestled in his mind, trying desperately to remember his given name.

Graeme excused himself to turn in. There were early morning chores to do, and it was getting late. Aenghas stepped out on the porch for a last taste of the pipe. James and Daegan joined him.

James was perplexed and uncomfortable. Aenghas had noticed it. James leaned against the railing. Daegan, sensing his torment, told him of his meeting with Elam Atwell. The man that was to deliver the horses was Thomas.

"You look a lot like him, but different," he said. "You have a gentler way about you. It seemed to me that Thomas had had a rough life, much by his own choosing, I think."

Aenghas struck a match and puffed on the pipe until it glowed red. He blew a smoke ring and sat silently for a moment. He hoped that by this account, the young man there on the porch would find himself again.

James pondered his childhood days. He replayed the pleasant memories and vividly saw his parents' faces. They were always happy in those thoughts. He heard their voices calling for him and his brother. But the only name that he could register was Thomas. He ran his hand through his thick hair, shaking his head in frustration.

"It will come to you, son," Aenghas said quietly. "You are a good man, I can tell you that." The night breeze blew through the chimes. They tinkled briefly. A night bird called, and all was quiet and still. After a long pause, Aenghas said, "Come now, boy, let's turn in. I'm guessin' you'll need your strength before this is all over." He got up and emptied his pipe ashes in the flower bed.

"You know, when I got home from town, I was surprised and delighted to see those horses standing in the corral. I was getting a bit concerned," Aenghas said. "They are finer than Daegan had expressed."

"Where's my bay?" James said, as a vague image began to reshape his thought.

"What's that, m' boy?" Aenghas asked.

"My bay? Where is he?"

"Don't know about a bay, son. You just keep on thinking, and it'll all come back to ya."

XX

The stagecoach finally rolled into Carter a half hour late. Vic and Dex were leaning against the saloon wall when the colonel and the reverend stepped down. The colonel gestured for them to stay put for the time being. He dusted himself off and gave them a quick nod. Vic and Dex eased their posture and went into the saloon. The colonel and the reverend continued on to the hotel where they asked for rooms facing the alley. The room the colonel chose was situated close to the back stairs.

He went in and took off his waistcoat. "Perfect," the colonel said. He was well armed, with two pistols strapped in shoulder holsters and a pair of pearl-handled Colts on either hip. He stretched out on the bed, crossed his legs, and propped his head in his hands. "Seems like a mighty fine town. I may just stay on a bit." He chuckled.

At sundown, the reverend tapped lightly on the door.

The colonel strapped on his guns and donned the waistcoat and fedora. He admired himself in the mirror before stepping out into the hall. The plan had been to meet at the saloon for a game of poker, but a good meal was the first order of business.

He entered the café with a swagger of self-confidence. His cane clicked on the floor with every step, as if to herald his approach. Every eye turned to look at this regal figure as he strode slowly to the table at the back of the room. Shortly, the reverend stood at the door and looked around. He chose a table that was close to the colonel. After the proprietor brought coffee, he struck up a casual conversation. All the patrons seemed to be engulfed in their own affairs and took no more notice of the two strangers. After dinner, they left quietly without the pageantry of the entrance.

The saloon was a bustling establishment. Vic and Dex sat at the back, engaged in a lively game of poker. The colonel and the reverend pushed the swinging doors into the room and quickly surveyed the crowd. Vic gave them a nod and shifted in his chair. He was going to clear the table. He had bided his time in the game, but now he would start the winning streak he could control almost at will. It didn't take long before the locals took what little money they had left and bid the strangers good night.

Vic rose from his chair and offered it to the colonel. The reverend gestured to Dex to move. Reluctantly he gave up his chair in the corner. That left Dex with his back to the door. No gunman willingly took that position.

Sensing his disgust, Vic laughed. "I got yer back, Dex."

"Thanks, Vic," Dex said sarcastically.

"What of the Parson?" the reverend wanted to know.

"Killed him," Dex said confidently.

"So, how'd you do it?" ask the colonel, skeptical of this empty claim.

"It was a pretty long shot, but I hit him in the head, I think," said Vic.

"Did you go and make sure, or are you just assuming he's dead? " questioned the colonel. "He's a crafty fellow and I have a feeling this isn't over yet. "

"The buzzards circled over him pretty quick and those other horses scattered. 'Cept that gray one. Jes' stood there," Vic retorted irritated at the colonel's criticism.

"Shoulda put a bullet through that one too," said Dex.

"Just the same, I'd like to have it for my own," said Vic. "Maybe I'll go back out and get it."

"All right. Do what you gotta do, then head on back to Collyre and meet up with Reynolds and Dobbs," the colonel instructed. "Thurman is in jail, so we'll have to get him out soon. Wait there.

We'll stay and see if the parson *does* show up. I'm going to check out a few business prospects. We'll take the train back next week."

After a few more hands, the colonel threw in, downed a shot of whiskey, and excused himself from the table. "It's getting late, gentlemen."

The reverend wasn't far behind.

The sun rose bright in a sky of clear blue. The storms of the past few days had freshened the landscape and cleared the air. After a good breakfast, the colonel went to the bank to inquire of land or business availability. He met the sheriff on the boardwalk.

Davis Edwards had been the lawman since he'd come to Carter some years back. Being in the military together, he and Mat had often been sent to detain criminals and prepare them for court, as well as to carry out their punishments. After they retired to civilian life, they had come west in search of quiet places where they refined their talents. The military had provided them with an education in law enforcement. They both were blessed with good common sense and a knack for justice according to the crime. They made no excuses and were not easily intimidated.

Davis was a good judge of character. He was wary of strangers and made it a point to speak with them about their business in Carter. He had gotten the telegram from Mat about some bad men coming his way. As of yet, he hadn't seen them. He used this coincidental meeting to inquire of the colonel's business and that of his friends.

"Howdy," he said politely. "What brings you and your boys to town?"

"Why, Sheriff, I am Colonel Dosiere from east of the Great River," he said. "I've come on official business of finding a certain man who gunned down one of my deputies some months back." He pulled a poster from his waistcoat and presented it to the sheriff. "Have you seen this man?"

"Hm, the Parson, is it?" Davis said, handing the poster back. "Can't recall seein' him. Do you know his given name or any other alias?"

"I'm afraid I was not given any other information about him," the colonel admitted.

"Hm. Well, I'll keep an eye out for him, too," said the sheriff. "How long you mean to stay?"

"Well, I actually like it here. I may just stay on...after I catch this rogue." He extended a hand. "Good day, Sheriff."

"Good day to you." Davis shook his hand. "We have a quiet town here, sir," he said as he tightened his grip on the colonel's hand and clapped his shoulder. He released the grip and tipped his hat. The colonel stepped by and crossed the street.

"By the way!" Davis called. "I am Davis Edwards, Colonel Dosiere." He watched the colonel enter the bank. He had seen this colonel before and now had to figure out when and where. There was something about Colonel Dosiere that struck a sour chord.

He went to his office and shuffled through posters, letters, and telegrams from other lawmen. He'd had dealings with this man. He was sure of it. It could have been, perhaps, when he was still in the army. He pondered his days back east in the military. So many of those times he had tried to forget. Now, here was this smooth-tongued fellow who spoke with a sticky politeness that irritated him. There was nothing in the drawer full of papers that entitled any law-man the authority to arrest him. There were no other strangers in town besides the colonel and his men. He would watch this bunch closely.

XXI

After a few weeks of recuperating from his clumsiness, Dobbs had grown aggravated and testy. Reynolds still found it difficult to breathe. Thurman continued to shout obscenities in jail. Mat kept the door shut to muffle the sound. The residents of Collyre went about their business but became increasingly irritated at the insolent behavior displayed by these so-called lawmen, temporarily living in their relatively quiet town.

The stage returned from Carter with a mail bag, Delores the school marm, and two strangers. Even though the townsmen minded their own business, everyone took notice of unfamiliar travelers.

Delores took her satchel quickly and scurried to her cabin at the schoolhouse.

Dex called, "We'll be seein' ya soon, ma'am!" He clapped a hand on Vic's shoulder. "Buy ya a drink?" He chuckled and shouldered his saddlebags. They carried their saddles and gear to the hotel and rented rooms.

In the saloon they began to drink and fester over the ill turn of events. They cursed their friends for the disadvantage they had incurred by misfortune and error. They had to spring Thurman from jail somehow. Reynolds and Dobbs were of no use, really.

As they sat at the corner table, Mat stepped through the swinging doors. They shifted as he looked directly at them. He walked over to where they sat. Dex had a hand on his pistol. Vic pushed his chair away from the table.

"Don't get up," Mat said sternly. Staring at Dex, he continued, "You! Hands on the table where I can see 'em. You boys anxious for trouble? I'm a mite short on patience, so just tell me your story. Then you can go back to your drinkin', and maybe I'll be satisfied."

"You got our partner in jail. You got no call to keep 'im," Vic blurted out.

Bart and a few hands from the Ballard ranch worked their way around the room to back the sheriff's play. Bart jacked a shell in his rifle and held it at the ready.

"Well, now, ain't that so?" Mat mocked their arrogant tone. "You wanna join 'im? I'll oblige ya right now."

Vic drew back and relaxed his posture, resting his arm on the back of the chair.

"I hear from our school teacher you put a fright in her on the way from Carter," said Mat. "You say you're the law? Lawmen don't b'have that way. You boys keep out of trouble, ya hear? I'll be watchin'."

"Why, shore, Sheriff," Dex said with a sneer. "We got all kinds o' time. Don't we, Vic?" Both men chuckled as the sheriff and Ballard's men backed out of the saloon.

They didn't waste any time, however, concocting a plan to spring Thurman. Dobbs was healing and in less pain but still had little use of his hand—his shooting hand, which made the aggravation that much more intolerable.

It was decided that they would use Reynolds's injury to get close to the doctor. She would be the leverage needed to persuade the sheriff to release Thurman.

"How we gonna get past the big fella?" Vic said. "He's always with her."

"We'll jest have to get at her when he's away...or kill 'im." Dex gave his partner a sly grin.

"We'll have to keep real quiet. No guns," Dex whispered as he drew his knife and began to pick at his fingernails.

They watched Whit's routine and waited for the right moment to make their move. They checked on the horses regularly at the livery.

Dudley fed at the same time every day, since Tuck was still hiding out. The boy was curious at the strange behavior of the liveryman but kept to his duties without question. The new strangers were rude and demeaning when they came to the livery. Dudley complied with their every whim, hoping they would just go away, and soon.

Then their chance came. Elliot Simms waved the telegrams as he scurried to the sheriff's office. "These came after that big storm hit," he puffed. "There was so much commotion, I plum fergot it, Sheriff."

"Hm," Mat grunted after reading the message. "Davis has some trouble with that colonel fella. Aenghas is looking for horses? Don't know about any horses. Tuck was mumblin' somethin' about some colts on the train. I wonder. . . Thanks, Elliot."

He decided to make the trip to Carter for the harvest celebration and lend a hand to Davis. The colonel had become overbearing, revealing his true nature, as the days slowly passed. He and the reverend weren't convinced of the pompous claim Vic and Dex gloated about. They proceeded to accuse the whole town of hiding this mongrel they had sworn to be rid of.

Whit agreed to watch the prisoner in Mat's absence. Clayton stayed with Miss Mallory while Whit was at the jailhouse.

Vic made his way to the doc's with an arrogant swagger. He knocked quietly on the door and waited until Clayton answered.

"Reynolds has taken a bad turn. We need the doc to come to the hotel right away," he pleaded.

"Why not bring him here?" Clayton asked.

"He's just real bad. We can't move 'im."

With that, he backed off the porch, quickly turned, and hurried toward the hotel. Clayton went inside to fetch Miss Mallory. He checked his gun and handed the doctor her shawl. They headed to the hotel together.

They went to the room where the injured men were staying. Clayton knocked on the door. The door, being ajar, creaked as Clayton drew his gun and slowly pushed it open and stepped inside. Mallory followed him. At once a heavy blow sent Clayton to the floor. Vic clamped his filthy hand over Mallory's mouth before she could call out. Just as quickly, the door shut behind them. Mallory struggled to no avail. Clayton lay lifeless on the floor with a gash on his head that bled freely.

"You're comin' with us, little lady," Vic chortled in her ear.

Tobacco drool dripped on her shoulder, his breath reeking of rotten liquor and cud. Mallory turned her head farther away, grimacing, nauseated at the stench and disgusted by the filth that enveloped her.

As she wriggled to get free, Vic threw her onto the bed face-down. His heavy hand pressed without mercy on her back. She finally resolved to her fate and lay still. Tears filled her eyes but she uttered no sound. Fighting back the urge to show fear, determined to survive, her thoughts whirled frantically, searching for a way of escape.

Vic opened the door and checked for any movement in the hall. All was quiet. He stepped out, holstering his revolver.

"I'll meet you back of the jail. I'll get the horses," he whispered to Dex.

Dex tied Mallory's hands. Throwing her shawl around her to cover her hands, he motioned her to the door. Wide-eyed, she stared in horror at Clayton as he lay bleeding, motionless, and then she stepped out the door with Dex pressing a gun into her side. Reynolds and Dobbs followed them. They made their way down the back stairs to the alley. It was late afternoon, so there were few people on the street. Their passing didn't raise suspicion as they made their way to the doc's office. Once inside, they proceeded through the kitchen and out the back door. Following the alley to the sheriff's office, they paused at the back of the jail where Vic was waiting with the horses. Thurman shouted to Whit as Dex eased his way to the boardwalk, and quietly opened the door and stepped inside. With the stealth of a great cat, he drew his heavy blade as he crept closer to the cells. Dex heaved the knife, burying it, deep into Whit's back before the big man could turn and spurn the attack. His heavy frame fell in a heap, life's spark evaporating from his eyes as he breathed his spirit away.

Heart-broken, Mallory sobbed when she heard Whit's body fall to the floor.

Soon the men emerged from the jail and mounted the horses that waited for them. They spurred their horses to a gallop, heading south just as Thomas had.

A dog barked wildly as the thunder of hooves echoed in the street. Bart ran out of the café, rifle in hand. He quickly maneuvered toward the raucous affair and fired a couple of rounds at the fleeing villains. A cloud of dust whirled about and concealed the riders as they sped away. Mallory managed to squeal enough to ignite a wave of rage through Bart's soul. He raced to the hotel to find Clayton staggering down the stairs, blood crusted across his face.

"They took her," he said. Weakness overtook him again.

Wellinger rushed from behind the desk and caught him just before he fell down the remaining stairs.

"What happened?" Bart snapped at Wellinger. "How did that foul scum get Miss Mallory? Did you hear anythin' from upstairs?"

"No, Mr. Bart, nothing at all," Wellinger said. "I had stepped away for about twenty minutes, you know, had business to attend to. It must have happened then."

At that, Bart stormed out and rushed to the sheriff's office, where he found Whit's lifeless form slumped against the cell bars, the prisoner gone. He pounded his fist on the door frame, then turned and ran to get his horse.

Now he was in a fix. He mounted his horse and whirled around, cursing at the swirling dust. He spurred his horse to the livery. Dudley ran out of the barn when he heard the horses race off. Bart stopped short of running him over.

"Go quickly to the ranch and roust the men!" Bart yelled. "I'm going after those scumbags. They took Miss Mallory, and I don't want them to get away. They're heading south into the dunes. Tell 'em to hurry. Tell 'em to hurry!" He shouted galloping away.

Bart raced away from town in pursuit of the men and Miss Mallory. His face was contorted. He was enraged at this bad turn. He had always watched out for his sister, Mallory, but had never wanted to smother her adventurous dreams. Now he'd come to regret his negligence. His horse labored through the deepening sand. The wind swirled the dust in giant curls, nearly erasing the tracks he desperately followed. He slowed his horse to a walk. Despair crept into his weary mind. Determined to save her, he focused on Mallory's sweet face and gentle touch.

* * *

The desperation in Bart's voice sent a chill down young Dudley's spine. He saddled Tuck's roan workhorse and lumbered to the ranch as fast as it would carry him. The horse was foaming and heaving when they arrived at the ranch headquarters. Mrs. Ballard left the laundry she was hanging on the clothesline, calling to her husband as she rushed to the young man. He slid from the big horse's back and panted the news to the cowhands who now surrounded him. Mrs. Ballard brought Dudley a cup filled with water and bade him to sit on the steps of the porch to gain his senses once more. The great horse hung his head and stood trembling.

The men ran to fetch their horses and lit out as quickly as Dudley had ridden into the yard. Dudley regained his strength and walked the horse to cool him down before offering him water. Darkness now came upon them. Mrs. Ballard urged Dudley to stay for the night and fixed him a slight meal. The guest room was prepared, and Dudley accepted the offer.

He lay awake, burdened with grief at the grave events that had unfolded so quickly. Dudley rolled onto his side and faced away from the window, covering his head. He finally dozed but was haunted by the faces of wicked villains forcing themselves upon Miss Mallory.

Waking to the brilliant sun shining in the window, he jumped out of bed, suddenly aware of the time. He splashed cool water on his face to soothe his eyes, swollen from the sorrow he'd felt in his dreams. He pulled on his boots and ambled out to the kitchen, still pulling on his suspenders. His rumpled clothes and mussed hair amused Mrs. Ballard. She smiled and quietly chuckled at the boy standing before her. She offered him breakfast before sending him back to town.

XXII

With Mallory in tow, the five riders drove their horses along the dry wash, continuing to press farther south. Their plan was to put as much distance between them and the town before night engulfed the desert. They would ride into the night and double back to throw any foolhardy pursuer off their trail. At the southern edge of the mesa, they found a hardened trail that wound its way up the west side. They crossed over a narrow pass dropping into the desert once again. They held to a westerly course for what seemed hours. The horses, weary from the hard ride, slowed and finally stopped. They would go on no more. Vic pulled Mallory from her saddle and threw her to the ground. Her wrists burned from the ropes that bound her. She had no strength to argue, and lay where she had fallen.

"We need to leave her," said Vic through clenched teeth. Aggravation burned in his eyes at the thought of coddling a woman on the trail.

"Yeah, well, not jest yet," Dex said. "She's gonna come in handy, I reckon. There's a posse comin', you can count on it. When we get out of their jurisdiction, we'll give her to 'em, eh!" His wicked laugh caused Mallory to wretch and gasp, swallowing her fear that perhaps no one could rescue her. Passing a flask of whiskey, they bragged about shooting the parson.

Thurman became agitated at the thought of Thomas getting away. "You say you killed the parson? Well, how is it I watched the parson ride outta Collyre? Who was it you shot? It certainly wasn't the cur we've been trailin'." He cursed Vic and Dex for shooting the wrong man.

"What do you mean? You callin' me a liar? He got off the train at the ravine with that gray and two other horses." snapped Vic. "We killed 'im sure as we're standin' here."

"Call it what you want. He left Collyre ridin' that big bay we been trailin'. Rode right by the jail. I seen 'im plain. Don't know who you shot, but it weren't the parson. We just got to git outta here, right now. We'll settle up later," Thurman hissed.

They camped in the cold desert to rest their weary mounts. The night was dark beyond comprehension. Malice grew stronger in the souls of these godless cowards whose very existence could be summed up in the brutal exploits they reveled in. Vic glared at Mallory, flipping his knife into the sandy soil and burying the blade to the hilt. His ruthless grin tormented her as she sat curled up to keep warm and shield herself against these demons of society.

* * *

Bart rode until dark consumed the desert. He could no longer see what lay in front of him. He was ill prepared for the night. He shivered and dismounted. Standing in the vast wasteland of darkness, a shroud of bitter cold and loneliness filled his heart.

He cursed the dark as he led his horse along the wash he blindly followed. He gambled on the thought that he knew this country and terrain better than his opponents and hoped to catch them before daylight. He knew of a broad path leading west at the southern end of the mesa. He hoped his guess was right. Perhaps he could get to higher ground and gain the advantage.

"Their horses are tired, too," he thought. "They will have to ease the pace some. We've got to keep going." He patted his horse's foaming neck.

Before crossing the pass, he would veer north and climb the mesa. It would be a steep trail, hard for his horse to navigate, but it was the only way to save Miss Mallory. He stumbled in the dark for the better part of an hour. Finally, the mesa rose up out of the desert floor. He groped along, searching for the trail that would take him to the top, when an owl jumped out of the brambles and silently flew away. His horse spooked, jumping backward, knocking Bart off-balance. To his surprise, the trail he had been looking for opened up before him. He chuckled to himself and thought at once about Ma Parker. He had never believed in all that stuff she concocted but was thankful for this "coincidence."

He decided to rest for the night and get going when there was better light. Pulling his coat tight around him, he huddled in a small crevice. He wished he had been better prepared.

* * *

Ballard's cowhands reached town and found some of the men carrying Whit's body out of the empty jail. They carefully laid him in the buckboard to take him to the undertaker. The women sang softly and wept as they drove away. Whit was a kind man, larger than life itself. No man could take him, except with a knife to the back. What would Miss Mallory do now that he was gone?

It was getting dark. The cowhands stayed in the hotel planning to leave at first light. They reasoned that it would be impossible to track either Bart or the murderers without sufficient light. They sat around a table contemplating a strategy, trying to calculate the direction the murderers would have taken. They decided to split their ranks to cover more territory. There was a great wilderness to search. Hopefully the tracks would remain in the sand. This time of year brought sporadic rain and winds that could erase any trace of travelers, dashing their hopes of catching the rogues. Before turning in, the men gathered goods that they would need for the chase. They had stocked up on ammunition for their pistols and rifles. The general store stayed open so they could get the provisions for a few days' ride. The canteens were filled. With Dudley gone and Tuck nowhere to be found the men fed and watered the horses bedding them in the stable behind the livery.

At daybreak the men met up in the lobby and ate scones and drank coffee Wellinger had set out for them. They went to the livery and saddled the horses, preparing them for the arduous day ahead.

Clayton mounted his big yellow gelding, Diablo, and raced off to the south ahead of the others who mounted and spurred their horses to a gallop close behind. A light breeze began to shift the sand. Slithering and coiling along the banks of the dry riverbed, it hissed as it sifted and settled in the imperfect impressions left by passing horses. Here and there, the ground cracked, disturbing the patterns drawn in the wash. Distinct hoof prints marked the trail of the outlaws. Clayton slowed to survey the options before them. All trails led west, he thought. . .until they reached the Bullrim. As the posse drew closer to the mesa, they drew lots for the directions the divided groups would take. Clayton and his men would continue to follow the well-laid trail while the others would scout the trails leading south.

* * *

Light began to ease across the eastern horizon. The chill before dawn crept into Bart as a serpent slithers silently, effortlessly across the sand. He shivered and reluctantly got to his feet. He was stiff. He arched his back to gain some balance before he took a step to his horse. Stretching from side to side, he finally managed to walk off the soreness that had permeated to his bones. Daylight came quickly. He led his horse up the steep slope, hoping the loose rocks would not alert the rogue band to his whereabouts.

At the top of the mesa, he tied his horse to a shrub and belly crawled to the edge. Far below and to the west, a dust trail billowed. He cursed as he watched. He had not gotten there in time. Below him he saw the remains of a campfire that could only have belonged to those he now pursued. In the dark he had not realized how close he was to the outlaws. He now knew the direction they would take. Bullrim Canyon would stop them and force them to turn south. There were trails that could get him to the bottom, though treacherous.

Few men knew of them. It would be sheer folly to tempt the power of nature. There were other routes that perhaps would allow him to overtake them.

Against his better judgment, he mounted his horse and spurred him over the edge of the mesa. His horse gathered himself and eased down the steep slope, sliding on his haunches. After several minutes they reached the desert floor and galloped freely, racing west as the outlaws and Mallory had.

* * *

Vic grabbed Mallory by the arm and pulled her to her feet. She winced at the strength and cruelty of her warden. He heaved her onto her horse's back. With her hands bound, she gripped the saddle horn for balance. When everyone had mounted, they turned west at an easy lope. The sun had just tinted the eastern horizon. The morning star twinkled gaily at the tip of the waxing crescent moon. There was nothing before them but the vast sandy desert and clouds gathering to the west with a cool breeze wafting toward them, carrying the faint scent of rain. After a time, Dex pulled up and turned to check for pursuit. There on the face of the mesa, he saw a line of dust descending to the desert floor. With a sneering grin, he swore and spurred his horse to catch up to the others.

"They're on us, boys," he yelled, riding up to the lead.

They quickened the pace, hoping to lose the pursuers in the vast desert. Mallory lurched in the saddle as Vic jerked on her horse's lead line. She felt despair creep into her heart and weakness strip her of hope. Yet she found the strength to persevere, knowing that someone was coming to rescue her. The memory of Whit's face haunted her. Anguish and grief consumed her at seeing his eyes emptied of life. Her eyes welled with tears knowing a part of her soul was lost with her dying guardian.

"Whit, I miss you. I'm so sorry," she whispered, blinking to drive away her sorrow and tears.

* * *

Thomas leaned against the granite wall that towered above him. From this vantage point he could see at least forty miles north and west. His eyes drank in the sheer beauty of the desolate expanse. At the uttermost edge of the horizon, the snow-covered mountain peaks shimmered in the evening light. The thunderheads that loomed in the northeast were arrayed in various shades of crimson and amber wrapped around the swirling charcoal clouds. "Fire clouds," he remembered hearing Charley say. It seemed quite appropriate. Though he couldn't hear the thunder, lightning skipped and flashed throughout the menacing nimbus.

He thought about her family and hoped they had survived the doom that conflict so often bears. They were a hardy lot, he remembered. Her father was a cagey fellow, hardworking and honest, but tough in spirit and resolve. There were few families he remembered before he was hastily driven from the settlement so long ago. This family was precious indeed. He'd hated leaving them behind.

The little fire he built flickered, and popped flinging sparks into the air. Staring into the flames, he chewed on some jerky and pondered the trail that lay before him. He wondered how James had got along.

Off to his left, a rockslide drew his attention. The bay, alert to impending danger, shied and pricked his ears to the sound. A donkey brayed as more rocks toppled from somewhere above them. Thomas drew his pistol and waited. Around the corner, the pack-laden donkey ambled to the bay and stood quiet, taking the opportunity to munch the grass. Thomas edged along the wall toward the donkey, but the chuck of a rifle lever stopped him suddenly. He wheeled around to see the barrel of a rifle pointed directly at him.

"Now, you jes' drop that hog leg real easy, mister." The command came from the escarpment to his right side. It was the voice of an old man. As he obeyed, the rifle barrel began to quiver.

"Aw, hell," the voice said with a small degree of disgust. Thomas relaxed a bit, a wry smile crossing his lips.

"Come on in, old-timer," he said with a chuckle. He picked up his gun, checked the chamber, and set it in the holster.

A grizzled little man with bowed knees gimped into the camp, rifle pointing to the ground. "Never could hold this thing up fer too long," he said dryly. "Got bad shoulders from pulling too much of my own weight. Hoo." He chuckled. "So, what brings you out here, s'far from city folks? If'n you don't have a mule, yer gonna wind up outta transportation, son. Closest settlement is the Cedars. Nigh on a days' ride and no water 'tween here 'n there. Less'n a'course you know where to look." He had a mischievous twinkle in his eye. "There really ain't much there, jes' an old well and a fella that fetches the water fer a price." He gnawed on a wad of jerky, staring out across the desert. After an uncomfortable silence, he turned his gaze to the donkey eating contentedly by the bay. "Aw, don't go there. It's a waste o' yer time," he said gruffly.

"I been here, oh, twenty year, now," he continued, trying to recall some story to justify how his life had turned out. "Don't see many strangers hereabout. Fact is, yer the first man I seen fer a long while. Well, that ain't exactly so. Jes' got back from over in Carter. Never did see it any busier than jes' last week. Seems some new fellers got off the train there, a couple of gun hands. Some dandy gents got off the stage, too."

Thomas felt a shudder deep within him. They'd caught up with James, and now he was in danger because of it. "Any chance you've seen anyone that looks a bit like me?" he asked the old man. "My brother was supposed to meet up with a fella in Carter about that long ago."

"No. No, don't recall seein' anyone else of note," the old man said.

Thomas, relieved at the thought, confided more in the old man. He told him of the run-in he had had with some bad men some time back. The old man listened without interruption.

At long last, the old man scratched his beard as he pondered the predicament Thomas found himself in. "Well, son, seems to me you best be gettin' there perty quick if'n you want to help yer kin. Reckon he don't rightly know what's about to befall 'im. 'Less'n 'a course they already got 'im."

Thomas was silent at the thought. He just couldn't bring himself to believe it, not just yet. He knew James was clever enough. He had to hold to his conviction and remain committed to the plan. There was nothing he could do but hope Ma Parker had shown James the way, as she had said she would.

The old man slapped his knee as a thought burst out of him. "I'll get you to Carter by the short cut," he said. "It'll be hard for your horse, but he looks like a determined feller. 'Sides, they git along." He nodded at his donkey. "Jes' be careful ya don't drift too far north, or that ol' Bullrim will swaller y'up. Strange river," he said, adjusting his hole-ridden hat. "I'll go with you a ways jesta make shore you get headed in the right direction."

"This is a strange country," Thomas said.

"Yes, yes indeed. Man stays long enough, you jes' become a part of it."

Thomas nodded and chuckled in agreement as he gave the old man a sideways glance.

"I like this here spot. A fella can see for miles off there," he gestured with a wave of his gnarled hand.

They settled in by the fire talking long into the night of bygone days. Before long Thomas began to drowse at the monotonous voice of the old timer sitting on the other side of the fire.

A chilled wind blew across his face that woke him. Blinking away the sleep, he realized it was morning. The old timer was setting the pot of coffee on a fresh fire.

"Mornin' to ya," he clucked cheerfully.

As he spoke, a wisp of dust caught his attention, making him sit forward as if to get closer. Thomas saw it too. With three long strides Thomas went to the bay and pulled an eyeglass from the saddlebag. He searched the direction of the dust but couldn't make out what was causing it. It could have been a number of things. It was moving quickly—maybe wild horses or people on the move. The thought occurred to him that it could be the men that pursued him. Then he saw them. The heads of men bobbing up and down with the rhythm of galloping horses. He peered harder through the lens at the last rider, who seemed to be flopping much like a rag doll. He cursed as he realized it was a woman. And not just any woman. It was Mallory. He pulled the glass down and closed it quickly. The makings of a plan began to take shape, though he couldn't bring his thoughts into the clear. Behind the settling dust, there came a lone rider in pursuit of the outlaws and Mallory.

Thomas knew what he must do, even if it was unwise. He must go after them. Without a word, he turned and tightened the cinch, grim thoughts clouding his better judgment. Stepping into the saddle, he turned to the old man. "The woman they have will not survive this ordeal. I fear the men that have taken her are the same that pursue me." With a strange and wild look in his eye, Thomas chuckled. "Won't they be surprised!" Leaving the old man to his imagination, he spurred the bay down the trail out into the desert.

"I'll jes' wait here a spell!" the old man called. "That young'n is fixin' to get tangled up with a snake. Shore hope he can get the jump on 'em." He tottered over to the donkey, whose ears pricked forward as he watched the big horse driving fiercely over the sand beyond the safety of the thicket.

"Never could understand why a man would risk anything fer a woman. They're nothin' but trouble, if'n ya ask me." He loosed the pack. The donkey shook in relief as the weight left his tired shoulders. He began eating, again disinterested in the world beyond the shelter and grass.

Thomas leaned forward to give the bay stud the full measure of rein. He rose out of the saddle to allow the great steed the freedom to run with the sweeping stride of his breeding. The sand dunes tested his endurance and perseverance. His nostrils flared as he heaved up the dune, digging in to gain ground. At the top Thomas pulled his mount to a halt to regain a sense of his direction. He looked back at the granite wall to gauge the distance he had covered. The bay's legs trembled from the exertion of the last mile. They walked on while Thomas calculated the options set before him. He had taken out so quickly, he had no time to formulate a plan. There was no sign of the riders. He had to find their trail and follow as quickly and silently as possible.

"Who was the last rider?" He wondered. "He couldn't have been with them, but someone in pursuit."

He must find this man first. Two apart could only mean disaster for Mallory. With that thought, he rode on in search of the trail the lone rider had left in the ever-shifting sand.

XXIII

Ma Parker huddled by a small fire at the back of the cave that would serve as her refuge from the colonel. She was not prepared to face him yet, but face him she must. She would pick the time and place, for advantage had to be on her side. She found new hope in the brothers that happened her way, and she was eager to help them vanquish the vermin that now disrupted all their quiet lives. As frightened as she had been, she now focused all her energy on helping these young strangers.

She sat entranced by the fire. Staring into the flames, she began to whisper a lyrical verse in an ancient tongue, crumbling dried leaves and thorns into the flames as the methodic ritual continued. The fire danced and swayed, seemingly on command. The blue flames burned to red-hot. A gust of wind entered the cave. The twisting flames swirled with fiery tongues licking the ceiling, igniting seams of a sticky black goo. The embers sizzled and spit in response to the hypnotic rhythm of her soft voice. The walls of the cave seemed to moan unexplainably. The fire cast shadows on the walls of gyrating phantoms from her past. She took up a jagged shard of obsidian and scratched out pictures of galloping horses, flocks of birds, and swirling dust devils amid sporadic bolts of lightning. As she drew the images, she chanted with deep menacing bellows and tingling shrieks of warning. The scavengers flew into the shallow cave, squawked, circled the fire, and furiously left in erratic fashion, beating their wings on the sides of the cave. Their calls drifted away as they flocked to the west, black feathers drifting gracefully to the floor. Then all was silent. Blinded by the welling up of her memory, she continued the incantations long into the night, until exhaustion overtook her.

She woke with a start to the clap of thunder. A sense of anguish and dread washed over her. The rain poured down, covering the opening to the cave as a veil. Her head hurt. A trickle of blood ran down her brow. She didn't remember hitting her head, but felt dazed and numb and found it hard to think clearly. How long she had been unconscious she couldn't tell. She had lost all track of time.

The thunder moved eastward. The pounding rain drifted on, giving way to a dreary dawn. A stream of water from somewhere above trickled into the basin at the edge of the cave. She drank from the bowl chiseled in the stone from countless years of runoff after storms. The water was cold and refreshed her. She bathed her throbbing head and crawled to the edge of the cave to look out on the rain-drenched desert.

The glare of the first ray of sun on the east horizon flashed in her eyes, blinding her. The sand glittered as the sun shone bright through breaks in the gray clouds.

The warmth of the late morning chased the remaining fog from the draws, she rubbed her eyes to clear the blurry film that seemed to distort her vision. There, far below, was a lone rider moving with an easy gait to the south. She raised her hands and gestured to a gust of cold air. It twirled and danced until it barely kissed the ground and skipped across the man's path. The scavengers appeared from nowhere, squawked, and flew erratically with the whirling sand. As quickly as they reached the rider, they vanished in a warm breeze. The rider stopped abruptly, searching the mesa for answers to the mysteries of such a strange land. He rode on. Ma Parker watched until he disappeared beyond the horizon. She returned to the small fire to warm her cold fingers. She ate a little, contemplating what could happen next. Though she could not see into the future, she could only guess at the logical sequence of events.

Later in the afternoon, the sound of distant gunshots reached the cave, and she scrambled to the edge of the cliff. She extended her vision and thoughts to town and sensed something had gone terribly wrong. Not long after the sounds of the gunfight ceased, there came the riders, spurring their horses into the desert. She gasped in disbelief as she recognized Mallory with them. After a short time, she watched as Bart pursued them. She recognized the flashy horse he always rode. It had a long stride, and the thunder of its hooves could be heard even at such a distance. Returning to the little fire, she stoked it with sage. The flames answered with a rushing wind, heating the cave in an instant. The dry leaves sizzled, sending sparks wildly into the air, where they fluttered to the ceiling before extinguishing into ashes that drifted to the floor like gray snow.

"I can only hope he understands my intentions," Ma said aloud as she stirred the red-hot coals that remained, releasing more sparks into the air.

Crumbling leaves of a bitter herb into the coals, she became entranced, mumbling another ancient poem. The hours ticked on, and still she recited the verses while the embers, now glowing softly, filled the cave with wisps of smoke and the scent of lavender and sage. As she uttered the last word, the shadows of night enveloped the cave. When all was silent, an owl hooted quietly in the distance. Ma Parker collapsed with exhaustion and slept.

XXIV

The posse met up again at the bottom of the mesa. They came upon the makeshift camp the outlaws had left. The fire pit was cold, but the rocks that lined it still felt warm.

"Not more 'n half day's ride, I s'pect," Clayton said aloud.

The ground was a jumble with so many tracks, but all seemed to leave toward the west. Off to the side of the trail were the tracks of one lone horse moving at a great speed. Clayton thought that would be Bart's horse. The men mounted again and quickened their pace. They were anxious to catch up before the outlaws got too deep into the sand dunes. Without fresh mounts, they would soon find themselves in danger of losing their horses and perhaps their own lives. After a time the men pulled up to consider the situation and discuss any ideas on how to proceed. They agreed that the outlaws would most likely end up in Carter. They decided to return to Collyre, board the train, and get there perhaps before the outlaws. They were reluctant to make the choice, because Mallory and Bart would be left to the elements. Clayton was bent on continuing the pursuit. He took extra water from the men and bid them good-bye. They would meet again in Carter. With that he jogged his horse along the trail Bart had laid before him. The rest of the posse rode slowly back to town.

"They will have to slow down, too," he thought. He hoped to catch up to Bart before too long. The sand dunes closed in around him. He had only been this deep into the desert a few times. The constantly shifting sand skewed his memories of the landscape. He felt as if he'd never been here at all. After a time, there loomed in the distance the great spire of rock that stood as a beacon on the horizon. It gave him comfort that he now recognized something in this unfamiliar desolation. He began to hear the rush of the Bullrim as he rode southwest. Still the tracks led ever deeper into the sandy desert, farther away from his companions. In the clear light of day, his hope lay with finding Bart and Mallory. There was the certainty of conflict awaiting him. He must not falter now, but be decisive in his actions. His senses were alert and he grew all the more wary.

The tracks seemed to be more distinct. He was getting closer, but dusk was approaching. Reluctantly, he stopped the chase.

He started out again just as light filtered across the silhouette of the horizon. He rode along following the tracks left by the horses yesterday. Staying just below the crest of the dunes, he dismounted and crawled to the crest for a better peek. He lay close to the ground, removed his hat, and peered over the edge. In the distance, he saw Bart lumbering along the sand, leading his horse. The tracks he followed continued on across the vast waste, an ocean of white sand as far as the eye could see. Just as he slid back to his horse, a shot rang out. He scrambled back up the dune to investigate. Bart had run for cover. His horse sprang away as sand exploded underneath him. Clayton lunged down the dune to his horse, who shuffled nervously. He mounted and turned to pursue Bart's fleeing horse. He knew Vaquero wouldn't go far, and if he saw a familiar horse he may just come back to him. It was a gamble, but the yellow horse he rode was Vaquero's pasture mate.

The men they pursued were now close and would be easy to track, and Bart couldn't be without a horse in this desolate land. They both needed their mounts. He crested a dune and saw the frightened horse, weary and struggling against the shifting sand. He gave a shrill whistle that brought Vaquero to a standstill. Trembling, he looked for the sound. With ears pricked toward Clayton, he slowly turned and quietly walked to the yellow horse. He nickered softly, licking his lips in relief. Clayton took up the reins and worked his way back to where Bart had been hiding.

138

Another shot rang out. Clayton quickened his pace, feeling the urgency of the moment. Keeping to the bottom of the dunes for cover, he urged his horse into a lope. He came to a scrub brush near the point he had left. He tied the horses and let them rest while he edged closer to the fight. He crested a dune and watched as Bart belly crawled to change his position. Still, he couldn't see the men who fired at Bart. The wind sent sand hissing off the crest of the dunes, blurring the ever-shifting mirage on the horizon and blowing dust into the air that glistened in the afternoon sunlight, sifted, and settled below the wind's reach.

After several minutes of silence, he chanced a peek over the dune again. Bart lay on his back, checking the rounds left in the cylinder of his revolver. Clayton belly crawled over the crest of the dune and down to his cousin.

With a big grin on his face, Bart greeted Clayton. "Hey, glad you could make it. I thought I was going to have to be a hero all by m'self."

"Ah, you know me and parties. Just can't stay away if there's gonna be fireworks," Clayton said, reaching out a hand to Bart. "Do ya think they've moved out?"

"Don't know, but Mallory can't keep up this pace fer long. She's got grit, but this lot ain't gonna be too compassionate, I'm afraid." Bart shook his head in disgust and swore under his breath.

"I got the horses over yonder," said Clayton. "Maybe we should ease over to them and try to flank those galoots. If we head east along the dunes, maybe we can get the jump on 'em before they get too much farther."

"Yeah, okay. It's worth a try. This country is too open to do anythin' else."

They slid back down the dune and crawled to where the horses were tied. They headed east along the bottom of the dune. They found that the farther east they moved, the more the dunes pressed them away from the men they pursued, farther away from Mallory. They mounted the horses and rode south, across the dunes. They would have to chance being seen to make up time. Time was against them and against their beloved doctor.

XXV

Thomas heard the gunshots but couldn't see the uproar. He spurred the bay in the direction of the shots. In the distance, he watched as two riders continued toward the south while four men lay atop a dune firing in the direction they had just come.

There must be a posse closing in," he thought. He used the distraction to pursue the two riders heading south, since most certainly Mallory would be one of them.

They would need water and soon, as hard as the horses were being pressed over the dunes. The old man confirmed Whit's suggestion about the Cedars. That would surely be the place to intercept them. He was hoping his hunch would be right. He rode south, thinking he could get to the Cedars before them.

After a long ride, the ground began to harden. It was level with more vegetation. The solid ground was a welcome relief to the tired horse. Sage brush began to give way to scrub cedar trees. Their fragrance filled the air with the cool breeze. Reaching the edge of a knoll, he looked out across a wide valley of green grass growing among more cedar and pine trees. There was a well-worn trail along the bottom. He could only surmise that it would lead to the refuge of the Cedars. Dropping down the hill, he stayed within the shadow of the trees.

He stopped and carefully scoped the grounds around the cabin at the head of the draw. Smoke billowed from the chimney. Two horses were tied to the hitch rail. Three others stood in the corral, lazily swishing their tails at the flies that pestered them.

He left the bay tied to a pine and out of sight. Concealed among the trees, he hurried to the cabin. Two men were arguing about the price of water. The sound of a woman whimpering could be heard amid the shouts and cursing. A gunshot ended the argument, and the woman screamed.

"No one's gonna hear you out here, so jest you shut up, now!" the man shouted.

Thomas shifted his position to get a jump on the man when he stepped out. He would have to shoot first, he thought, and forget any of the questions he needed answers to. The sound of rustling feet inside the cabin moved closer to the door. A chair tipped over with a thud. He heard the commotion of the woman struggling to get free of her captor, but to no avail. A heated rage erupted within him when he heard the distinct sound of a fist striking Mallory's cheek and her falling to the floor. He burst through the door, unable to stifle his anger any longer. With guns blazing, Thomas shot three bullets into the villain's chest. Vic stumbled forward, falling face down, at his feet. Holstering his pistols, he hurried to see to Miss Mallory, who lay unconscious on the floor. He gently rolled her over onto his knee. A bruise had already begun to swell under her left eye. He picked her up and laid her on the shoddy cot in the corner of the room.

He went to draw water from the well. "Guess it'll be free, today," he thought. "No one collecting the money."

That thought raised an eyebrow as he went back into the cabin. "Now, I wonder where that old coot stashes his money," he said, looking around for the earnings. "After all, it's not really stealin' if you take it from a dead thief." Walking around the room, he happened to step on a soft spot in the floor. It creaked and gave way under the weight of his boot. Lifting the rug, he found that a square of the floor was loose. Beneath it there was a strongbox, which he lifted out. There was more than twenty dollars in it. After pocketing the money, he returned to Mallory, who was beginning to waken. In the dim light she began lashing out at Thomas as he tried to subdue her and ease her fears with gentle whispers.

When Mallory regained her composure, they began to devise a plan to escape the rest of her captors. Thomas went out and saddled one of the horses in the corral. Then he let the others loose, including the one Vic had been riding.

Thomas convinced Mallory that they must continue on to Carter. It would be too difficult to go back across the desert dunes. They took what little grub was left in the cabin, and filled the water skins. They each had three canteens strapped to their saddles. Thomas tried to remember what the old man had told him about crossing the Bullrim. They headed west, hoping to make it to Carter ahead of the men who'd kidnapped Mallory.

* * *

Bart and Clayton rode out of the dunes and found the tracks of one lone horse. It was yet another mystery with no answer. They pondered which way to go, deciding that these tracks would lead to the Cedars. It was the only logical choice before them. After a time, they split up to look for the tracks of the outlaws they pursued. They met up again at the edge of the wide valley of lush grass, surrounded by a forest of cedars and pines. Their attention was immediately drawn to the cabin at the headwaters of the spring. There four men raced westerly on the trail that climbed out of the valley. Spurring their horses over the edge, Bart and Clayton pursued them. When they reached the bottom, they reined their horses to a stop in front of the cabin. There lay a man they recognized as one of the rogue outfit.

Clayton shook his head in confusion. "This whole thing is mighty peculiar, ain't it?"

"So who's got Mallory, then?" Bart said.

Surveying the horses grazing close by, he recognized the mount Mallory had been on. He started shouting her name in hopes that she was hiding somewhere near. When no answer came, they again raced after the men.

They were getting close. They could smell it. Anger welled up from deep inside their being. Bart felt his face flush with fury as he pressed Vaquero harder up the slope. Against his better judgment, he crested the hill. A shot ricocheted off a boulder not a foot from him. Vaquero reared as shards of rock peppered his legs nearly throwing Bart to the ground. Clayton stopped just short of the rim and dismounted, pulling his rifle from the scabbard as he hit the ground. The desert wind whistled through the cedars, but no more shots came. The dust rose from the retreating horses.

They regained their wits and scouted the jumble of tracks leading westward.

Clayton turned to Bart. "They can't continue this pace for too much longer. Those horses are gonna play out soon."

"The only place they can go is Carter," said Bart. "They'll have to cross the Bullrim. We may overtake them there. They don't know where to cross. I've been there once."

"Once?" Clayton asked.

Bart chuckled. "Yeah, it can't be that hard to remember. When I see it, I will know it."

"I hope you find it sooner than late," Clayton said with a wry smile. He cursed and mounted his horse. They headed west at an easy pace. Now they had a plan. Sort of.

XXVI

James was getting restless cooped up in one place. He was feeling a burden to the Dougans who had taken him in and continued to treat him as kin. His strength had returned, and did chores to help out, but still felt out of place.

The whole family prepared for a trip to Carter for the annual harvest celebration. The farmers and ranchers gathered there to share in the bounty of their fruitful labor. Little money was exchanged, as they instead traded and swapped vegetables for calves and lambs. Chickens and eggs would pay for bolts of cloth and other dry goods. Ailene brought the fresh milk from her favorite cow. Aenghas crated a young steer and loaded it on the buckboard. They had packed jerked meat and salted pork to trade for goods at the store.

James welcomed the invite with the excitement of a child at Christmas. He helped Graeme hitch the team of heavy draft horses to the buckboard. With the extra weight, their greater strength would be needed. Aenghas offered the gray mare for James to ride. He and Daidre rode behind the buckboard, while Daegan and Graeme led the procession. The day was crisp and clear, with no storm clouds to dampen the festivities. They traveled at an easy pace.

As they neared the town, Charlie came running out to meet them. "There was a telegram that came for you not long after you left last week," he said, extending the folded note to Aenghas.

Aenghas read it frowning, perplexed. "Who is Nathan Navarr?" he wondered aloud. "Whit is completely daft."

"Did you say Whit?" James asked. "Why do I know him?"

"Well, Whit is from Collyre," Aenghas said. "You were there, remember. It says here that James was to deliver the horses. Is that you, son? Maybe this Nathan fella is really Thomas. Must be some trouble comin', for sure."

"I reckon so. Sounds a mite familiar. If I look like Thomas, it must be as you suggest." His memory suddenly became clear. "He is riding my bay stud. Now I remember. There are men after him. They must be closing in. I reckon there's gonna be big trouble."

They decided James should hold back and hide the mare outside town. There was a shaded draw with water and grass to tether her for a short while. James would walk into town after dusk, when the festivities moved to the livery for the dance.

The town was abuzz with all the activities of the celebration. James waited patiently until the sun began to set. He was getting hungry. He worked his way through the draw and scouted out how he could sneak into town. Then he noticed Graeme loitering at the side of the livery barn making his way over to the outhouse. When he came out, he dropped a wad of paper near the edge of the gully. After he had gone, James crept to the place where the paper lay.

"*There is a man layin' wait for you,*" the note said. "*Calls himself a colonel. There's a preacher man with him. Somehow I don't think they do much but look the part. Be careful.*"

The big red barn had been cleaned out. Bales of fresh, sweet straw lined the stalls in rows like benches. Quilts were laid neatly over them. The soft glow of lantern light filled the big room. Sawdust brought in from the mill north of town covered the floor. The gents each brought an instrument, either guitars or fiddles. They took turns at making music for the dance. There would be no tinny piano tonight. Clay jugs were used to keep time to the reeling of the fiddles. Everyone began to file into the barn. The forge in the corner was aglow with a gentle fire to heat the large space against the chill of the autumn night. There would be storytelling and merry music for the last few hours of the celebration.

A lean-to stood next to the hay shed. James led the mare quickly up the draw to it. Once she was settled in, James eased his way through the shadows to watch the festivities from a ways off and to look for this gentleman who sought him.

* * *

Thomas and Mallory could hear the Bullrim as they neared the mighty river. Thomas wished the old man was around to help him find the crossing. It could be days before he found it, if it could be found at all. The horses were tiring, as they were themselves. There was no cover for them to rest, and night was deepening. Mallory finally could go no farther.

"Please," she pleaded. "I have to stop."

"Okay," Thomas said. "We have to push on soon, though, or those men will catch us. Do you know anything about this river we have to cross?"

"No, I've never had the desire to venture this far from Collyre. And now, without Whit..." Her words fell away to her sobs of grief.

"What do you mean? What has happened to Whit?"

"He's dead! They killed him when they got that bad man out of jail. I was so afraid that I would be left to die, too."

Thomas took her in his arms and let her cry into his chest. He searched his heart for some words of comfort from the only truth he knew to be absolute. A bitter hatred welled up inside him. He was torn between knowing right from wrong, yet knowing what he must do to right the injustice wielded by evil demons preying on innocent souls.

He prayed for wisdom, strength, and mercy. He knew he had to change the course of his life as well as Mallory's. He eased Mallory to the ground and held her until at long last she slept. The night was dark. The moon had followed the sun and set at dusk.

The chill that comes right before dawn awakened Thomas. He roused Mallory.

"We've got to move on. Are you ready enough?" he said. "Let's just walk a ways to get some stiffness out, okay?"

Mallory stood and stretched. "Okay, I'm better now. Thank you," she said. She drank from the water skin Thomas offered her. They started out just as a rose hue kissed the eastern horizon. The morning star winked and twinkled at the coming dawn. It soon would be swallowed up in the brilliance of the new day. They crested a ridge just as the first rays of the sun shone into the valley that spread before them. There below was the Bullrim, wide and glassy, rippling to the south. The roar of the north fork could no longer be heard. Thomas scouted the shores for a way across. Out of nowhere came the squawking of many scavengers circling wildly. Several had landed in a lone cottonwood tree on the other side of the river. Thomas let out a hardy laugh and shook his head in amazement.

"Is there nothing Ma Parker ain't aware of?"

Mallory was perplexed. "Whatever do you mean, sir?"

"Those birds there. Every time there is somethin' to pay attention to, they show up out of nowhere." He laughed again. "That must be the crossin'."

"You're going to believe a bunch of old crows?"

"Yes. Yes, I am. C'mon, now, have a bit of faith." Thomas headed down the gentle slope to the water's edge.

Mallory followed, still skeptical.

They mounted and eased the horses into the river. It was boggy at first. The horses struggled to keep from getting stuck in the mire. Thomas spurred the bay to keep him moving. They lunged forward a few more strides until the bank gave way to the depths of the river. As the bay began to swim, Thomas slid from his back and held to the cantle. Mallory followed him. The current pulled at her skirt as she struggled to hold tightly. She lost her grip and slid into the current. She held desperately to her horse's tail. The current was relentless, and Mallory fell into despair.

"Hold on, Mallory," Thomas called to her. "We're almost there. I'll get you out. Don't give up now."

Mallory reached deep within her very soul. Her fingers hurt. She tightened her grip and let out a wail of anguish, but still she held tight. She wanted only to reach this man she could possibly trust and live for.

Safe on the western bank, Thomas looked back across the river. There on the hill were four riders. "Hurry, Mallory, they've caught up to us. " Thomas helped Mallory onto her horse. "We've got to find a place to make a stand."

They spurred the horses into a gallop. Hearing gunfire disturb the quiet of the morning, Thomas looked behind them toward the commotion. The shots were directed at the four riders, who scattered and searched for some cover. There was none to be found. The scavengers flocked together and flew wildly north and out of sight.

The deadfall of an old forest and boulders was strewn before them. Thomas and Mallory reined in the horses and quickly dismounted. Thomas grabbed his rifle and lay behind a fallen tree.

The gunfight continued. They were too far away, but Thomas waited for any opportunity to engage in the fight. In a moment, the shooting stopped. The four men lay dead. Their horses scattered. Two men stood on the hill. They slowly moved among the fallen men. Thomas didn't recognize them.

"Do you know them, Mallory?" he asked.

"Why, yes, I do," Mallory said excitedly. "That is my brother Bart and cousin Clayton. They must have been the ones chasing the bad men."

They mounted again and headed back to the banks of the Bullrim.

As they drew near, Bart and Clayton rode down the hill to the riverbank.

"It's pretty boggy there!" Thomas called across to them. "Just keep 'em moving, and you'll get to the deep part. That current is pretty strong. Hang on tight."

As the men finally made it to shore, they greeted Mallory and her rescuer.

"So this is the answer to the mysterious tracks we seemed to cross for the last couple of days," Bart said, extending his hand.

"Well, I don't know how mysterious I am, but I had a good vantage point and couldn't let things go as they were," said Thomas. "I thought we were in for a difficult fight before you came along. Guess that makes us even. The name is Thomas Atwell." He extended his hand to Bart.

"How'd you find the crossin'?" Clayton asked. "We didn't rightly know where to begin." He chuckled and gave Bart a sly glance.

"Well, there were those—"

Mallory cleared her throat, making him pause.

"Well, I mean, it just looked like a good place to cross. We didn't have much time to be picky. Don't know if it's the best crossin' or not. But we made it, didn't we?"

"Carter ain't too far now," Bart said. "I'm getting pretty trail worn. Could use some grub from the café there. And some coffee."

"Yeah, and Diablo is just about done in, too," Clayton said.

"Well, we'll be obliged to ride along with you," Thomas said as he reached for Mallory's hand.

The snow on the far west mountains stood in the violet haze of the evening's fading light when they at last crested the hill and saw in the distance the glow of a settlement that could only have been Carter.

XXVII

The barn was filled with harvest revelers. There was lively music and boasting aplenty. The women brought out a feast of turkey, potatoes, and pies. A hog farmer had roasted a pig in a large pit outside, where he had tended the coal bed all day. The aroma filled the air when the meat was ready to carve.

The colonel strutted around the festivities as if he had orchestrated the event. Being a stranger, however, he was ignored and brushed aside as a fly might be. His indignation boiled. Finally, he approached the sheriff inquiring again about the man he and his "posse" pursued.

"There are no strangers in town besides yourself, Mr. Dosiere," Davis said. "You and that preacher man."

The reverend puffed up and stepped toward the sheriff with his hand reaching for his gun.

"Now, there is no call to get defensive, sir," the colonel said, pressing against the reverend's play. "We're here to see justice served. We have time."

The reverend relaxed his stance but glared at the sheriff with a vehement stare.

James found his way to the barn and settled into one of the stalls, out of sight of the main party. Daidre brought him a plate of vittles and sat with him.

Just as they were finishing the last bites, the reverend strolled to the edge of stall, gun in hand. "Never did believe that misfit could take you. I knew you'd show up, you cur," he said with a sneer. "Get up and fill yer hand, or I'll cut you down where you sit."

"Be careful what you wish for," said James easing the plate onto the bale of straw where they sat. "You just might get it." He urged Daidre away to the corner, out of the line of fire. She slid along the wall. The reverend pushed her down, demanding she stay still.

"This is between you and me," James said. "Leave her out of it."

"She's staying so you don't do anythin' stupid," the reverend said.

"You got the wrong Atwell, Porter," Thomas said as he shoved a gun barrel into the man's side. "Drop it, or I'll drop you, here and now."

The reverend dropped his pistol and turned to face the man who had eluded him and stolen his money purse. "So here we are at last, you and me," he said. "Seems the last time I saw you, you was hightailin' it while the brethren was seein' you off." He chuckled. "They just didn't want what you had to offer anymore."

"You deceived 'em, Porter," Thomas said. "You promised 'em things that you couldn't deliver."

"Yeah, they were so easy. They'd have given me everything. I just told 'em what they wanted to hear. They didn't want to hear any of that spiritual stuff. They wanted relief and prosperity right now. It wasn't hard to convince a gullible horde that I had a direct line to God and in fact was one myself. The women were fine, Parson."

"You are a cold and heartless soul. You will pay for your treachery, if I have to serve the warrant myself." Thomas cocked the pistol. "Your friends have deserted you and will no longer be a threat. They're gone, killed and sent to hell just as you will be."

Just then, Davis stepped in. "Hold up there now, son."

Porter knocked Thomas's gun aside and dropped to the ground. He grabbed his own gun and fired. Thomas jumped out of the line of fire. The bullet found a true mark. Davis fell to the ground. Daidre found refuge behind the bale of straw as James pulled his gun and engaged in the fight.

At last, it was over. Porter, the reverend, lay dead. Daidre rushed to the sheriff's side. He was not gravely wounded but would need time to heal. Mallory dashed into the livery and looked at Thomas and James, wide-eyed. Realizing they were safe, she then turned her attention to the injured lawman.

The crowd of revelers had gathered at the door of the livery. Mathias Winston pushed through the crowd, gun in hand. To his relief, his friend was alive. The colonel strode into the room. His eyes grew wild when he saw Porter slumped in a corner, unmoving. An old crow with one white feather in its left wing perched on the rafters of the livery. It called out a long, low squawk.

"Where is the maroon[1] to whom that crow belongs?" the colonel shouted. "Where is the witch? Her eyes are as hollow as the bowels of the earth. Her heart is as cold as the ice at the very peak of the world. She will be the death of us all!" He raised his cane as if to strike the foul creature.

"Best pay attention, Colonel," warned Thomas. "She means for somethin' to happen to you. You know those scavengers come around when she sends 'em. Might be best for you to move on, sir."

The colonel's face grew pale. Reduced to humiliation, he steadied himself with his cane and backed out of the livery. The train was leaving in the morning, and he would be on it. This was a pitiful land, he deemed, but wouldn't be conquered by the likes of him.

* * *

The train whistle blew shrill, shattering the silence of dawn. The colonel boarded alone without fanfare, defeated. His strong arm had been crushed by a desolate land and insipid ignorance, as he saw it. The train lurched and began to chug eastward. He soothed his aching spirit with the flask from his jacket pocket.

The train, at last, entered Collyre. Tuck stepped into the passenger coach and offered the colonel a quaff of liqueur, then vanished as

---

[1] runaway slave

quickly. The colonel drank of it and felt a warm surge rush through his head. For a brief moment, his memory was strikingly clear and in the distant corner of his mind, the image of Martha Parker, the woman whom he had searched for, in vain, devoured his last fleeting breath. He looked out the window and recognizing the woman with an old crow on her shoulder that opened its wings to reveal the one shimmering white feather. He dropped the flask, realizing that he would crave, for eternity, release from her haunting apparition. His head fell forward. The colonel was dead, forever shackled, in torment, with the searing chains of his insatiable evil. An ominous cloud of noisy scavengers swirled and flew away ahead of a dust devil that twirled and danced on the warm breeze.

Time passed, the seasons changed, and the storm clouds dissipated . . .

Life had finally settled into what it was meant to be. Thomas saddled his horse and rode out into the desert loping freely at an easy pace. The sun rose warm and bright in a clear blue sky. When they reached the mesa they followed the game trail that wound upward to the cave where he and James found refuge from the evil that had pursued them. It seemed so long ago. He dismounted and sat on the broad ledge reflecting on the course his life had taken. The sketches on the wall depicted two brothers driven apart by selfish differences, uniting, at last, in an unforeseen destiny. Among friends they found solace and companionship in this place of opportunity. He came to the realization that this is where he belonged, concluding that burning bridges can be mended after all.

Mallory marveled at the iridescent evening clouds dressed in violets and pink hues. A warm breeze wafted from the west, sweet with the fragrance of fresh spring sage, tousling the tresses of her yellow hair. Lingering with anxious anticipation, she cupped her hands over her eyes searching the wide prairie for a glimpse of the man who promised to return to her.

Character Profile

Thomas Atwell (Tom "Parson" or Nathan Navarr, Prophet Navigator)
James Atwell
"Reverend" Porter
"Colonel" Dosiere
Ma Parker (Martha)
Mathias Winston
Mr. Morris (storekeeper)
Tuck
Mallory Murphy
Whitton Tarver
Louis V. Ballard
Mrs. Ballard
Bart Murphy
Clayton Knox
Reynolds
Thurman
Dobbs
Vic
Dex
Norris Atwell
Mary Atwell (Mother)
Elam Atwell
Simone Atwell (Aunt)

David Atwell (Uncle)
Eustis Atwell (Grandfather) ('Preacher")
Esther Atwell (Grandmother)
Aenghas Dougan
Ailene Dougan
Daidre Dougan
Daegan Dougan
Graeme Dougan
Daeniel Dougan (Smithy)
Maitilda Dougan (Maiddie)
Dudley
Mrs. Mueller
Davis Edwards
Charlie (Telegraph agent in Carter)
Elliot Simms (Telegraph agent in Collyre)
Stanley Wellinger (Hotel clerk)
Charley (a little girl from one of the settlements where Thomas preached)
The Old Timer
Man at "The Cedars"
Delores (School marm)

The Atwell family was a diverse group of individuals. They owned a thriving apple orchard. Grandfather Eustis began preaching at an early age after an apprenticeship with a preacher that was well established but wishing to retire from the pulpit. After a few years of struggle, the Atwell sons wished to move out to the frontier and try farming. They sold the orchard and began planning for a new future. Eustis gave the money from the orchard to Norris and Elam as their inheritance, which they promised not to squander. Uncle David became a gunsmith, building the weaponry used in the war. When they finally made the decision to move on, Mary was pregnant, unknowingly with twins. Simone was a tremendous help to her sister-in-law. Elam and Simone had two children of their own, but Thomas and James were older by that time. The family prospered for a time until the rumor of conflict reached their doorstep. The boys now were growing up and began to develop their own personalities. After an insignificant difference of opinion, they went their separate ways.

Mallory Murphy was born into an affluent, aristocratic home. It was difficult for women to attend college but because of her family's influence she was accepted to the medical school and graduated in the upper echelon of her class. When she was in her teens she was attacked and beaten as she walked home from a class. Had it not been for Whitton Tarver, she would have surely been abused further and possibly murdered. Whit was a vagrant who just happened by. He had been a pugilist and the property of a gambling man that fell to a reckoning by an "associate." Whit had fled, vowing to remain a free man. Mallory's father was so grateful that he took in her rescuer and felt indebted to him for life. When Mallory completed her medical training she and Whit moved to a small town beyond the Great River to begin a new life. Whit was her constant bodyguard and companion.

Mathias Winston and Davis Edwards had been in the military together and had studied law. They moved west when the frontier was lawless and crude. They sought to bring civility to the territory beyond the Great River. There were two towns that they visited and ultimately settled in, Collyre and Carter. They remained in contact with lawyer friends back east and relied on their contacts to alert them to the migration of outlaws that fled the consequences of war. There seemed always to be drifters passing through, due to the fact that the railroad passed through Collyre and ended at that time in Carter. The lawmen knew that at some point the railroad would continue beyond Carter, and progress would bring good folks as well as the discards of a contrary society.

Lou Ballard and his hands were cattlemen. Lou built his herd from gathering the strays of the wild cattle from the southern plains. There was good pasture and agreeable climate just northeast of Collyre. He settled on the open plain and staked a claim on a large tract of land. He was a hardworking rancher with integrity and loyalty to the right side of the law, as were the men that rode for his brand.

Bart was Mallory's brother, while Clayton Knox was their cousin. They came west after Mallory to try their hand in the cattle business. Lou gave them a job just as soon as they got off the train.

"Reverend" Porter was a storyteller. So convincing were his tales that he soon began quoting scripture when it suited his grander scheme. Oftentimes he sat in the back of the tent listening quietly as Thomas preached, and then he would find a point at which to turn the community against Thomas. As Thomas would flee, Porter would step in as the spiritual leader and soon gain the misguided trust of the colony. He found that in desperate times people would reach for any solution to their ill-fated and dismal circumstances. He was a charismatic, smooth-tongued snake that took advantage of the simple-minded people. When he had taken all they had, he would move on, leaving the colony all the more destitute and humiliated. He knew one day he would face Thomas for a reckoning once and for all.

Reynolds, Thurman, Dobbs, Vic, and Dex were solipsistic[2] misfits that were recruited into a rebellious service as assassins during the civil conflict. They were the consequence of prostitutes and pirates that were prevalent on the southern coastal regions of the country. They reveled in terrorizing the peaceful society living on the frontier, robbing them of life, liberty, and valued possessions. They grew up in an orphanage but all too gladly ran away to join the lawless and learn the art of being trained killers. Their callous, dark hearts reeked of the evil that devoured them, stealing their knowledge of right and wrong. They were "brothers" only in that they lived together at the orphanage. They were without mothers and fathers and held no allegiance to any cause. Their conscience seared, robbed of decency and compassion, they filled the black void with their own insatiable greed and hatred, which festered all the more when one of their own was gunned down by a Bible-wielding drifter.

The Dougan clan had immigrated to the New World from across the ocean. They brought with them the revelry of music and shaggy cattle to build a new life for their family. They settled on a majestic valley along the Bullrim River. The pastures were lush and green, nourished by the cold waters that flowed lazily alongside them. The land seemed to rejoice at the very presence of a happy, hearty steward. Aenghas and Daeniel were brothers that had married sisters

---

[2] extreme egocentric

from the McLaughery clan. Daeniel moved into town and set up a blacksmith shop and livery. The family remained close despite the distance from town to the ranch. Aenghas became impassioned with horse racing. News of the endurance of the thoroughbreds east of the Great River had reached the farthest edge of the frontier. He purchased the beginning of a herd of horses that were swift and "long winded."

Dudley was a young teen who was infatuated with the railroad and loved to travel back and forth between Collyre and Carter. The railroad tycoon gave him a job simply because he was always riding the train anyway. The pay was enough to help his widowed mother make ends meet. He was an honest, jovial lad.

Stanley Wellinger had been a butler for a prominent family in the east. His employer moved to Collyre and built the only hotel in the town. Wellinger managed the business while his employer moved back east. His family did not fare well in the wide-open spaces.

Mrs. Mueller settled at the Northford station, providing a place of hospitality for the stage lines. There the roads going east, west, north, and south converged.

Charlie had been hired at the telegraph office since he knew the code used to communicate over the wires. He was a small man but had a keen sense for the dahs and dits clacking at the telegraph table. He taught Elliot Simms the art of telegraph coding.

Ma Parker (Martha) was a young girl when her family came to be the possession of an aristocratic cotton planter. Her family had ties to the slaves on a large island in the gulf south of the mainland and were among the many that had run away during a Class Revolution that began in 1791. The "maroons" (runaway slaves), as they were known, had escaped to another republic of this island and made their way to the continent beyond the great gulf waters, where they quickly found themselves in bondage once again.

There was a man Ma's family knew only as the "Colonel" that came to the plantation on regular visits. He was suave and debonair, proud of his aristocratic heritage, also linked to citizens of the same island. Though he denied it, his descendents had the combined traits of the elite class and domestic servants, known as "mulattos." He charmed Martha's sister. He became enraged one night when he found her with another man. He killed them both and began to pursue Martha. She was terrified of him and ran away, since she had seen his rage firsthand. She escaped into the swamp, stumbling upon the "Bayou Witch," who took her in and protected her with incantations and sorcery. She lived with her for many years and learned the art of pressing oils from the wild herbs growing abundantly in the marshy soil. After the old witch died, Martha ventured out of the swamp and headed west. She met up with a man that was suffering from a snake bite. She healed him and they continued together across the Great River. Tuck remained her loyal companion. The venom as well as the herbs she used to heal him had muddled his wits. He had an odd demeanor and chased invisible demons in the night.

There always seemed to be a flock of scavengers circling overhead. One particular raven would sit on the log beside her. She fed it the scraps from her plate. It had a long white feather on its left wing that seemed to shimmer when danger was near. It responded with clicks and squawks, bobbing his head as if nodding in agreement while she talked to it of her plans. She vowed that she would lay to waste the man who had killed her sister. She had haunting dreams of meeting him one day, knowing she was destined to kill him or die trying.

All the names and places are fictitious.

Made in the USA
Charleston, SC
01 August 2015